Benjamin's Secret Journal

Faith Kidz® is an imprint of Cook Communications Ministries
Colorado Springs, Colorado 80918
Cook Communications, Paris, Ontario
Kingsway Communications, Eastbourne, England

First printing, 2004
Printed in the United States
1 2 3 4 5 6 7 8 9 10 Printing/Year 08 07 06 05 04

Cover design: Marks & Whetstone
Design manager: Nancy L. Haskins
Cover illustration: Jeff Whitlock
Interior design: YaYe Design

Library of Congress Data applied for.

ISBN 0781440033

Secret Journals of Bible Time Kids

Volume 3

Benjamin's Secret Journal

Equipping Kids for Life

An Imprint of Cook Communications Ministries
Colorado Springs, CO

Faith Builder

Ages 9 and up

Hope

A Faith Builder can be found
on page 132.

*To my family,
whose love and support
have freed me to write.*

Contents

Stuck in the Middle

Hey, Journal,

Rabbi thumped the top of my head with his oversized knuckles. "Hello? Are you in there, young man?"

"Uh ... yes ... I mean, what was the question, Rabbi, sir?" I asked.

Our open-air classroom sits in a sunny spot near the entrance to the synagogue. It's easy to daydream on mornings like this, when sunshine and a cobalt sky lure me to the world beyond Bethsaida. My teacher is not one to give up easily, though.

"Benjamin, please recite today's Scripture reading," said Rabbi. He arched his bushy eyebrows before adding, "You are ready, are you not?"

I took a deep breath and recited the passage as fast as I could. In the front row, Peter's hand flew up as soon as I faltered. Peter catches mistakes like a frog catches flies.

I didn't panic—I'm used to Peter one-upping everyone in

class—I did what any cornered kid would do: I cracked a joke.

"Hey, did you hear the one about the boy who—"

Rabbi's eyes flashed a sharp warning. "Sit down, Benjamin!" He turned to Peter, who was waving his hand frantically. "Yes, Peter?"

Peter closed his eyes—he claims it helps him think—and recited the entire lesson without a single pause. I sized up the quirky shaggy-haired kid who seems so much smarter than the rest of us. How does he memorize such a long passage?

After class, I hurried off to avoid having to talk to anyone, but Peter caught up with me. "Benjamin, wait! I'll walk with you."

"How did you do that?" I asked him.

"Do what?"

"How'd you memorize all that Scripture overnight?"

"I just like to study, that's all. It's really not that hard."

"That's easy for you to say," I said, rolling my eyes. "I'm doing well if I can remember two lines of Scripture. *Seven* lines? Forget it!"

Peter shrugged. "Well, it just takes a lot of focus, that's all."

I knuckled the top of his head, Rabbi-style. "Ahhh, your parents must be so proud of their smart little boy!" I teased.

Peter studied the ground for a few seconds. "Yep. They would be proud if they could see me in action."

Peter might be quirky, but I can count on him to tell the whole truth and nothing but the truth. "Maybe you'd do better if you weren't so busy trying to be the funniest guy in class, Benjamin."

I dropped to the ground and pretended to writhe in pain. "Help! Please, someone help me—quick! I've been stabbed in the heart!'"

"Here," said Peter, offering his hand. "Get up before all the old ladies in town show up with rolls of bandages."

He nodded toward a row of houses. "Here's my turnoff," he said. "I'll see you tomorrow."

I continued on, but kept my eye on Peter until the hills swallowed him up. He and I are from different worlds. I crave the limelight; Peter craves knowledge. I don't give a care about preparing for class, but Peter studies hard and can be counted on for correct answers. He's a whiz kid, the shining star of Bethsaida.

As I neared my neighborhood, I overheard a couple of girls talking about their diaries. One of them was griping because her brother had stolen hers, and she found him reading her secrets. "He tossed it in the dirt and laughed at what I'd written," she said. "According to him, guys don't waste their time writing in 'stupid' diaries."

Well, of course guys don't keep diaries! Diaries are for girls! But there's nothing wrong with keeping a "journal." A journal is just a record of stuff that happens that's important to me. So what if some of it isn't exactly public information? That doesn't make it "girly"! Besides, it seems like my problems shrink when I write them down. Sometimes I tell my journal things that I wouldn't breathe to anyone. It feels good to spill my thoughts, sort of the way it feels when I talk to God.

Hey, Journal,

Long before I reached the last house on the left, I heard my sister's squeals.

Six-year-old Lydia tumbled into the street and ran to meet me, yelling, "Benjy's home! Benjy's home!" Lydia is a human whirlwind, a sweaty tangle of skinny arms and legs in constant motion. "C'mon, Benjy! I'll race you home!"

Mama greeted us at the door. "Such dark circles under your eyes, Benjamin. Are you feeling alright?"

"I'm just tired, that's all," I said.

She eyed me suspiciously. "Did you recite today's lesson?"

"Sort of," I said.

Mama's frown hit its mark. "It's important for a boy to learn the Scriptures, Benjamin. A man of knowledge is respected by everyone."

The men were due home from the Sea of Galilee soon. Mama sat at the table, slicing and dicing vegetables for our evening meal. She slid an onion across the table to me. "Here, give me a hand."

Lydia stared longingly at the onion. She dreams of the day when Mama will let her handle a sharp kitchen knife. (Girls sure have weird dreams!)

"Don't worry, Lydia," I said. "Someday you'll get to chop all the vegetables you want. Just like someday I'll have a real job of my own."

Mama nodded. "It won't be long, son. Just ask your brothers. They used to moan and groan about the wait. Now look at them—out on the water every day, hauling in fish like old pros."

"When do you think I'll have a chance to prove myself?" I asked. "I'm almost thirteen, and I haven't been on Papa's boat once. Abe and Micah were invited to help when they were twelve."

Mama shrugged. "Ask Papa. He's the boss."

Ask Papa. Lately, that seems to be Mama's standard answer. Can't she make a single decision without Papa's advice?

"But I've already asked," I complained. "He keeps saying I'm not old enough."

"And, if I remember correctly, Papa advised you to focus on school. You've plenty of years to chase after a job later on, Benjy," she said.

"Mama? Could you please start calling me *Benjamin?*"

"Benjy, schmenjy. It's all the same to a mother," she said, squeezing a chunk of my cheek.

When is Mama going to let me grow up? I'll be stuck in the middle of this family even when I'm thirty. Hopelessly stuck!

Mama read my sour expression. "Get over your poor-me's and give me a hand, Benjamin. Papa is bringing a few of the crew members home for dinner, and we need to set an extra table."

The men's long shadows arrived first, spreading across the street like lapping waves. They arrived dirty and tired, full of fishing stories and hot air.

"So tell me, Benjy, how's life in boring Bethsaida?" asked Abe.

"That's *Benjamin,*" I said.

"How's school? Are you still entertaining the class with your charming stories?" Micah winked at me.

I'm so sick of their teasing! I used my most powerful weapon: I ignored them.

Papa tackled me in a hug. "I've missed you," he said. "Tell me what you've been up to."

"Three words," I mumbled. "Study, study, study."

"I know, son. It's tough right now, but work hard at it. Someday you'll be glad you did."

Hey, Journal,

After dinner, the crew sat around our small patch of grass like they were ornamental plants, bragging about their week's catch. They're an exclusive club of fishermen and aren't very welcoming of outsiders. Will I be able to earn a seat in that circle of comrades someday?

Then again, what if I decide I don't like fishing? Do I have to become a fisherman simply because my grandfather, father, uncle, and brothers make their living on the sea? I wonder how Papa would react if I decide to become something else—like a potter, a baker, or a scribe? What would he say if I want to tend flocks like cousin Timothy?

The fishing life has changed Abe and Micah. Neither of them have any free time to explore the hill caves with me, or write messages on the beach with a stick like they used to. I almost have to make an appointment to talk to them! I don't dare tell Papa this: The life of a shepherd sounds much more intriguing. A shepherd works in wide-open spaces, not jammed in the middle of a crowded boat. I already get enough of this stuck-in-the-middle stuff here at home.

Late this evening, Papa poked his head into my room. "You awake?" he whispered. "How would you like to tag along with me to buy fishing supplies in Capernaum tomorrow? We'll leave early, so you'll be back in time for school."

I think Papa has a sneaky plan up his sleeve. Maybe we're really going fishing instead of shopping. Yeah—that's it! He's going to steal me away for the day so I can show my stuff—what I know about catching the biggest fish in the sea. The crew will be so impressed, they'll beg me to forget about school and join them instead. "Who needs an education in the Scriptures, with a talent like yours?" they'll say. "Surely God has blessed us with your presence!"

I agreed to go, but I pretended I knew nothing at all about his secret plan. (Why ruin a perfectly good surprise?)

Bonnie Bruno

Jackal in Capernaum!

Hey, Journal,

Papa and I awoke early and slipped out of the house. The neighborhood was dark, except for an occasional lamp glowing in a kitchen. Mama used to rise before dawn to start her bread dough, but no more. "A grumpy cook makes mistakes," she likes to say.

Our route wound around several fields of barley and wheat. Groves of figs and olives dot the land of wealthy property owners. Close to shore, we passed a row of fishing huts. There we followed a sandy path toward the shops of Capernaum.

At a point where the path steepens, I heard a high-pitched yipping coming from an overgrown area of dry grass. I inched over in the direction of the noise. A pair of yellowish eyes stared at me, surrounded by matted hair and teeth that looked like they could rip my arm off.

"Papa! Look—there in the weeds!" I shouted. Papa spoke in a quiet, firm voice: "Walk, don't run, Benjamin. He looks either sick or wounded. Hurt animals can be very dangerous, and we don't want to tease or provoke him."

"The poor guy is shivering, Papa," I said sadly, "and look— he's so skinny, I can count its ribs."

"Here, boy," I called softly. Its eyes softened momentarily. *It just needs food, water, and a little love,* I thought. I was wrong. Boy, was I wrong! The dog leapt to its feet and snarled. Its thick brown fur stood on end, like a creature from a nightmare.

"Forget the dog, Benjamin!" Papa practically dragged me up the trail.

"Papa, that was a jackal, I'm sure of it!"

Papa kneaded the back of my neck. "Everyone knows that jackals like more hilly regions; they don't live this close to the sea. Your imagination is working overtime, son—as usual."

Here we go again. Why does everybody think I make up these stories? If someone saw a lion lying across the entryway of the synagogue, the whole town would be talking. But who will believe a twelve-year-old who spots a jackal hiding near the seashore? Certainly not Rabbi, who was not going to accept any excuses for my tardiness.

I arrived back in Bethsaida a bit late, and decided to sneak into class. I tiptoed in and tried to take a seat next to the kid by the door. My plan fell apart when I tripped over the kid's books.

"Well, well, well," announced Rabbi. "It looks like our friend Benjamin has decided to join us. Would you like to explain why you're late?" asked Rabbi.

"I'm sorry, but I had a near-death experience this morning! My father and I ran into a jackal in Capernaum. It nipped at our heels and chased us halfway back to Bethsaida!"

Eyes bugged. Mouths flew open. I thought Peter was going to

pass out.

Rabbi seemed underwhelmed, though. "A jackal—in Capernaum, of all places? Why, I've never heard of such a thing! Remember what Scripture says about a lying tongue, Benjamin?" He directed me to move forward to a seat in the front next to Peter. "Perhaps you'd like to sit here, where I can keep a close eye on you."

Peter waited until Rabbi turned away. "Meet me after class," he whispered.

My teacher had other plans, though. At the end of the day, he said to me, "Wait right there, young man." I froze, and Rabbi stepped between me and the exit. "Here, have a seat." We sat facing each other, and Rabbi leaned in close to make his points. He spoke in short bursts, and each time he exhaled, the air between us shouted "Onions! Garlic! Fishcakes!"

Hey, Journal,

I still cringe when I recall Rabbi's words.

"I'm summoning your parents to a conference," he said. "You're habitually late, and I can't remember the last time you came prepared to recite your lesson. I do not recall either of your brothers showing up late for class, then trying to sneak in. Abe and Micah were naturals when it came to memorizing Scripture. I believe you're a natural, too, Benjamin, if you will apply yourself to studying."

Abe and Benjamin were *naturals?* What a laugh! If you ask me, they're just natural goof-offs. I mean, they're not dumb or anything, but they sure aren't the brightest lamps on the block, either. Besides, why was Rabbi comparing me to them or anyone else? Why can't I just be myself?

I couldn't stand it. I had to speak up. "Well, Rabbi, Sir, Abe and Micah aren't exactly the picture of success. Maybe they were good students, but they're just ordinary fishermen now. The last time I checked, they weren't rich or famous, either."

Rabbi's expression softened. He smiled at me through caring gray eyes. "Success does not rest on one's riches, Benjamin," he said. "It comes from the inside, from listening to God and obeying what he says. I'm afraid you don't have much practice in that department."

He cleared his throat as if to advertise his next sentence. "Because I want to see you succeed, it is imperative that I meet with your parents."

I wiped my clammy hands on my tunic. "Well, my parents are really, really busy, Rabbi," I said. "I don't think they'll be able to meet with you this year. I have to rush home every day to help out because my father is on the sea for days at a time. I'm not even sure when he'll be home again. My mother is busy with cooking and cleaning and caring for my sister, and—"

Rabbi waited for me to slow down. Why do I always blabber when I'm nervous?

"Enough, Benjamin! Let's focus in on the real issue here, shall we? I am concerned about your study habits," said Rabbi. "You are not applying yourself. I assign work, and half the time you ignore it. "

"Well, it's not like I haven't tried," I protested. "Last night, for instance, my sister interrupted me so many times, I couldn't even remember which passage I was supposed to be reading! It's hard to memorize anything under those conditions, Sir." (Rabbi likes it when we remember to address him as Sir.)

"Benjamin, Benjamin, it is time to face the truth. Your laziness is preventing you from learning at a reasonable pace. It is my job to train you in the ways of God. With your parents' help and support, I am confident we shall succeed."

I bowed my head and begged for mercy. "Rabbi, Sir, I'm really, really sorry. Please give me another chance! I'm not very good at memorizing, even under the best of conditions," I confessed. "Maybe we could try shorter passages. Yes! I think that would work!"

Rabbi is not a young man—far from it. Hundreds of boys have filed through his class over the years, some eager to learn and others—well, let's just say they were like me. Some adults are quick to label kids like me "incorrigible," but we're actually more inquisitive than the average person. I just happen to have questions, lots of questions! And answers, too.

"Sir," I continued, "part of my problem is that I have answers for the wrong questions, and questions that don't have answers."

An ever-so-tiny smile crept across Rabbi's lips. He waited while I recited my litany of excuses. "Are you through, Benjamin? Fine. Now, we are going to have to reach an agreement soon, or I'll have no choice but to speak to your parents. Agreed?"

I nodded so fast, my neck crackled. Was Rabbi softening? "I agree one-hundred percent and then some."

"Learning the Scriptures is a cornerstone of life," said Rabbi. "The wisdom of the ages is found in these lessons. Someday you will teach them to your children, just as your father and grandfather passed them on to you."

I wanted to ask how all those lessons would help a shepherd protect his sheep or a fisherman catch fish. Instead, I nodded and replied, "Alright, Rabbi Sir, I'll try harder. It's a promise. You have my word, like a big fat oath stamped across my forehead. You'll see, I really, really mean it this time, and if I don't—"

"Benjamin, take a breath," said Rabbi, patting me on the back. "'I'll try' is all I wanted to hear."

Wishy-Washy Fisherboy

Hey, Journal,

Last night I laid on my bed and repeated today's Scripture reading so many times I put myself to sleep! I need to show Rabbi that I mean business. Otherwise, he won't excuse me to spend a day with Papa on the boat next week. That's right; I'll soon be heading out to sea! My parents got their heads together and decided that if my schoolwork improved, they would speak to Rabbi about excusing me for two days.

"You're old enough to taste the life of a fisherman," Papa said. "It'll do you good to see what your brothers and I do all day. I haven't told Grandpa and Uncle Lemuel yet. I'll let you surprise them yourself."

Grandpa lives close to the sea in a house he and Grandma shared for over forty years. When she passed on, I thought he'd want to move in with us, but he insisted on staying put. He calls his view of the Sea of Galilee "a little glimpse of heaven." Spending time on the sea with the men of my family is going to feel like my own little bit of heaven, too.

Hey, Journal,

Sorry I haven't written in a while, but I haven't had time. School-work has taken up every spare minute. It paid off though; Rabbi now thinks I'm a genius. He called me "a gem that just needed to be polished." Hmmm. I like that—me, a polished gem!

Papa shook me out of a deep sleep. The house was pitch dark, except for a wide circle of light dancing on the ceiling above his oil lamp. "Benjamin, get a move on! We'll be leaving in half an hour," he whispered.

I hate being jerked awake like that, especially in the middle of a dream. "Leaving? Leaving for where?" I asked.

"A fisherman can't wait around for sunrise, Benjamin," said Papa. "If we hurry, we'll get to our secret fishing spot before the other boats have a chance to launch."

What's the big rush? The Sea of Galilee is hardly a puddle; there's plenty of water for everybody. I slipped yesterday's tunic over my head—no sense messing up a clean one—and grabbed the lunch Mama packed for me last night. Papa's crew were already gathered near the edge of the road, talking in hushed tones. The morning was unusually windy, with gusts that blew Micah's hat off more than once.

Walking alongside members of the crew, I felt older and taller—like one of them. Their language sounded foreign, though, laced with fishing terms I didn't understand. Papa winked and squeezed my shoulder. "Glad to have you along, son," he whispered.

"Thanks, Papa. It looks like I'm in pretty good company," I whispered back.

We arrived to find a crowd already gathered at the seashore.

Fishermen from other crews greeted us warmly, slapping long-term friends on the back. Grandpa let out a surprised whoop when he spotted me. "Well, look who's here! I figured you'd show up any day now," he said. "I'm just sorry you picked such a stormy morning for your first time out."

Fishermen milled around, discussing the risks of launching their boats. Darkness had not yet lifted, and I could hear the wind-driven water slapping against the shore. I stifled a yawn so the others wouldn't think of me as a sleepy weakling. I wanted to make a good impression on my very first day, or they'd never invite me back.

Uncle Lemuel—*Lem*, for short—jabbed me in the ribs. "So, what do you think of all this, Benjy? Should we quit yapping about the weather and get moving, or stay put?"

I cringed. Why does everybody insist on calling me that nickname? "Uh ... that's *Benjamin*, Uncle Lem. I'm almost thirteen, remember? And as far as the storm goes, I say we should go ahead and launch the boat and see what happens."

Micah and Abe raised their eyebrows. "Little brother has spoken," said Abe.

Even though our ages are several years apart, my brothers and I usually get along well. I ignore their show-offy remarks, which they only spout off when they have an audience.

I pretended to not hear and turned my attention to the horizon. A pale pink haze teased the point where sky met water. Soon we'd either launch or call off fishing for the day.

An older fisherman with a scruffy gray beard gave me the once-over. He questioned my father, as if I didn't belong there. "Hey, Mark, who's the kid, and why's he standing around with his hands in his pockets like a wishy-washy fisherboy?"

Bonnie Bruno

"That's my youngest son, Benjamin," said Papa. "I brought him with me today, to keep you in line."

The bewhiskered old crewmember responded with a long laugh, exposing a gap where his two front teeth used to be.

"What happened? Did someone punch him in the mouth?" I whispered to Papa.

"No, he fell overboard while trying to wrestle a fish into the boat. Knocked his mouth on the side of the boat when he tried to crawl back in."

"But didn't anyone help him?" I asked, horrified.

"Sure," said Papa, trying his best to look serious. "We helped drag him aboard. But first we sent him back into the water to look for his missing teeth."

I felt a shiver crawl up my spine, before Papa and the whiskery man burst into laughter.

Dark gray clouds slammed together in layers, casting a chilly shadow over the sea. The wind whipped the water into angry whitecaps. It didn't take an expert fisherman to predict Papa's news. We would not be leaving shore today. "The water's too choppy for fishing," he said, "but the day won't be wasted. We'll spend time checking out our equipment today."

"Here, give me a hand," called Papa. My brothers and I helped him spread a large fishing net across the sand—one of many nets that need regular mending. The hemp net was heavier than I thought it would be. We each worked in sections, checking out every inch of the rough net. Rock weights dangled from the bottom of one side, while the other side held chunks of lightweight cork. "The cork helps float that side of the net," explained Abe.

I kept glancing at the sea, hoping the wind would die down.

The water foamed and rose in a rhythmic, dizzying dance. *What a rotten change of plans! I finally get to join the crew, and look what happens—they put me to work mending nets instead of fishing. I'd rather be back in school.*

I found a few areas where stones had broken off the net. Papa handed me a long needle and a handful of rock weights. By drawing the needle and heavy thread through a hole in the middle of each stone, I was able to secure new weights in place.

"Good job for your first time at sewing," said Micah.

I heard someone snicker. "Looks like we've caught ourselves a live one! Way to go, Benjamin." It was the old bearded fellow.

Papa nodded. "Not bad, Benjamin. Not bad at all!" He showed me how to make a knot to anchor my first stitch. I looped and tightened each stitch to reinforce the new weight. A thought hit me suddenly: God does the same for me, too. He knows my weaknesses and finds ways to mend them. I wonder if he can mend my daydreaming ways, too? Rabbi wouldn't recognize me if I could get through a whole week without getting sidetracked.

Hey, Journal,

Tonight I made my bed in the corner of Papa's boat, sheltered from the wind. It's not the most comfortable place to lay my head, but hey—a fisherman has to do what a fisherman has to do, right?

I'm having trouble falling asleep. Don't get me wrong, Journal; I'm plenty tired, but I have a problem: I can't find the needles we used on the nets! Without them, I'm a dead duck. If I tell him I lost them, Papa will send me home. If I don't tell him the truth, he'll accuse someone else of losing them. And that wouldn't be right.

It's going to be a long night. I dread facing Papa tomorrow.

Nailed by Needles

Hey, Journal,

Ever since I was old enough to follow Papa around, I've dreamed of going fishing with him. I imagined how much fun we would have. We'd pack a lunch with all our favorite foods, and Mama would stand at the door and wave good-bye to us. Papa would buy me a new fishing pole, and show me how to bait my hook. I'd fish off the left side of the boat, and he and the older men would cast their heavy nets off the right side. Once I learned the basics, I'd graduate to the right side, where the men would praise me for catching the most fish.

Well, so far, my fishing dreams have been squashed like a bug under a sandal. Sure, we've fished at a couple of streams and ponds, but I've never awakened to the gentle rocking of a boat—not once. When Papa's business grew, he didn't have time to fish just for fun anymore.

I woke this morning with sunshine across my face—a good sign! *Maybe we'll get to actually fish today,* I thought. The sea was still and glassy, mirroring a flock of seabirds searching the water for their breakfast. "Don't get any ideas," I felt like calling out to them. "The fish belong to us today."

Papa jerked me back to reality. "Benjamin, I need to mend a tear on a net. Where'd you put the needle pouch yesterday?"

My stomach flipped as I searched for an answer.

"Brown leather, with a drawstring top. Does that sound familiar?" asked Papa, trying to jar my memory.

"Sure, it's right here," I said, tossing the pouch over to him.

Papa took one look inside and frowned. "The pouch is empty! Where are the needles?"

I hate the feeling of being pressed for information. It's not like I lost a family heirloom! The stores in Capernaum have plenty more needles where those came from, don't they?

"Can't we just buy more?" I asked with a shrug.

"Son, good needles aren't cheap, and we can't afford to leave them lying around on the beach."

Papa didn't give up. "Your carelessness is holding up the whole crew, Benjamin. We can't launch the boat until the equipment's gathered and stored away. That's the rule we live by. Now, find those needles and be quick about it."

Micah came to my rescue. "Come on, Benjamin. Abe and I will help you search." He found four big rocks and laid them on the ground like the corners of a square. "Let's spread out and cover this entire area. Those needles couldn't have just walked away."

Abe looked like he'd rather wrestle a badger than dig through the sand for the missing needles. "Micah, you're crazy. The wind shifted so much sand around last night, it's a wonder it didn't bury us, too. It'll take a miracle to find needles in all this."

"Nice try, little brother," said Abe, "but we're going to uncover them if it takes all day."

"Well, it better not take all day," muttered the old bearded fisherman. "We can't afford to miss another day sitting here on the beach. Look at all those boats on the water! We'll be lucky to find a spot to drop anchor this late in the morning."

Every so often, the crew glanced over to see how the search was going. I found the first needle at the perfect time, right when Mr. Whiskers was sighing and muttering for the umpteenth time. I held the needle up for him to inspect.

"The kid found one!" he announced "Hey, look—another one!" The crew broke into applause as we refilled the pouch. "Sixteen...seventeen...eighteen!"

"Papa, the pouch is full. Can we fish now?" I asked.

It's hard to think about what happened next, let alone write about it. I was beginning to feel like a real member of the crew, when someone bellowed seven words that changed my whole mood. "Next time watch what you're doing, kid!"

I swung around to protest, but came face-to-chest with a burly fisherman with a hairy chest and a smirk bigger than my head.

"Excuse me?" I replied.

"I said, 'Next time watch what you're doing.' A little pip-squeak your size has no business on the water if he can't even handle the basics."

I felt my face flush. *Papa, where are you when I need your support?* I heard myself mumble a feeble apology. "Sorry," I said. "It's was only my first day, you know."

Mr. Hairy-Chest leaned down close, eyeball to eyeball. I could smell his morning breath. "Today's your second day.

Let's see what you can mess up next." He threw back his head and laughed. Others joined him in laughing at the new kid. I felt like a baby.

A hand at the small of my back led me away from the crew. "Don't mind them," said Abe. "They have a way of making a man feel smaller than he is. You didn't do anything the rest of us haven't done before, Benjy."

"That's Benjamin. And I feel stupid no matter how many others have messed up."

"Well, Bigmouth forgets the time he dropped our entire load of bait overboard," whispered Abe.

My brother meant well, but nothing he said could erase my embarrassment. "I'm leaving," I said. "I don't belong here."

"You can't leave now," said Micah. "Once we're here, Papa doesn't let us off that easy."

"Benjy, you don't want to do that. Papa won't invite you back if you break the rules," said Abe.

I ignored my brothers and stomped off in the direction of home. *"It's Benjamin!"* I called over my shoulder. "B-E-N-J-A-M-I-N. Got that?"

A few minutes up the path, Uncle Lemuel's voice rang out. "Giving up the life of a fisherman so soon?" he called.

"Yep." I didn't feel much like talking.

"Can I help change your mind?" he asked.

Couldn't he see I was not in a talkative mood? "Hmmm. Well, you could give me three good reasons to stay," I said.

Uncle Lem caught up with me. "I have an easy answer: 1. Fishing. 2. Fishing. 3. Fishing."

"No thanks," I said and walked on.

I had pictured Papa's job as much different than what I

found. I thought he just fished all day. I never thought much about ripped nets or lost equipment. I figured he fished, rain or shine, and took his nets to someone in Capernaum for repair. And the men—I had no idea some of them were so gruff and mean! How could Papa enjoy going to work with a crew like that?

The life of a shepherd was looking more appealing with each step.

Hey, Journal,

Uncle Lem and I followed the shoreline until it reached the path back to Bethsaida. "We'll head back to the fishing camp in a couple of hours, after I gather a few supplies," he said. "If this weather keeps up, we'll have a good night of fishing. You'll love fishing at night, Benjy—oops, I mean *Benjamin.* And thanks to you, our nets are strong."

He slapped me affectionately on the back. "By this time tomorrow, you'll feel like a real fisherman."

I nodded but didn't reply. To tell you the truth, I wasn't really sure whether I wanted to become a "real fisherman" after all. Uncle Lem has a way of making silence comfortable, and we walked without speaking for the next few minutes. He was counting on me to return to the seashore with him. As much as I hated to disappoint him, I didn't see a need to make this trip last any longer. How can I let him down easy?

Bonnie Bruno

The Long Path Home

Hey, Journal,

When we neared Bethsaida, Uncle Lem spoke up. "Look, there's fisherman's row," he said, pointing to a row of ramshackle fishing supply shops. The shacks looked as old as the hills, weather-beaten but still standing. Two middle-aged men were engaged in a heated discussion when we arrived, waving their hands around and shaking their heads.

"You should have seen what happened!" cried the older of the two. "If I hadn't witnessed it myself, I wouldn't have believed it. Someone touched the hem—just the *hem*, mind you—of Jesus' garment, and she was healed!"

"It sounds to me like you fell for a bad joke," said the other, rubbing his whiskers thoughtfully. "Did he ask her for money?"

His friend shook his head. "No! Of course not! And it wasn't a joke! Still, I don't know what to believe. Some people say Jesus is the son of God. He claims his power comes directly from his 'Father.' Think of it—he has healed the blind and made the lame walk again. How could that be a trick?"

The whiskered gentleman threw up his hands. "And don't forget the guy whose hearing was restored. Imagine that—completely deaf one day, but able to hear his children laughing the day after!"

One of the shopkeepers stepped outside to see what the commotion was all about. "Who's to say whether it really happened? Do any of us really know whether those people received a permanent healing? How do we know they weren't paid to pretend they could hear and see?" His laugh sounded like thunder. "Pay me and I guarantee I'll sing and dance for you, too!"

The group broke up, but their conversation replayed in my head. I couldn't shake what I'd heard about this mysterious robed stranger. Jesus—Son of God? Healer of the blind and lame? Could it be true? I suppose nobody can know for sure, but what if Jesus really is God's own Son?

I was lost in a daydream when Uncle Lem emerged from the store carrying a bag of hooks, sinkers, and special thread for mending those pesky nets. "Hello ... calling Benjamin ... Benjamin, have you floated out to sea?" he crooned in my ear.

I jumped. "Oh! You startled me, Uncle Lem."

"Now what in the world could capture a young man's thoughts so completely—a pretty girl, perhaps?"

"Hardly! I was just thinking about something I overheard a while ago," I said. "It's juicy news, Uncle Lem. Want to hear it?"

"Sure, fire away."

"Well, one of those guys says he saw Jesus perform a miracle!"

"They must have been in Capernaum when Jesus passed through yesterday," said Uncle Lem. "The shopkeeper told me a similar story."

"Well, what do you think, Uncle Lem? Is it true?"

He didn't hesitate. "I believe it happened just the way they described, but I'd like to see Jesus for myself, just to be sure."

I tossed my uncle's words around for a while. If a person really, truly believes, why would he also need to witness something in person "just to be sure"? Isn't that like asking the sun to rise twice, to make sure it really went up there?

"I wish I'd been there to see Jesus in action, too," I said. "He seems to cause a stir everywhere he goes."

I helped Uncle Lem carry his fishing supplies, but almost dropped the bag when I spotted those two men again. "Look, Uncle Lem! There they are—those men I told you about. Ask them what they saw in Capernaum yesterday."

Uncle Lem is a polite man. He usually doesn't barge into people's conversations, but this time his curiosity got the best of him. He stepped into the growing circle of men as if they were old friends meeting to discuss the latest news around town. "I've never seen anything quite like it," said the older gentleman. "Someone touched the hem of Jesus' garment and was immediately healed! Truly, he is the son of God."

A young man standing off to the side muttered something and led his small child away. "Don't listen to that man," he told his little boy. "He's only telling a make-believe story."

"People will believe anything they want to hear," said another onlooker. "Whatever happened to telling the truth?"

I wonder what Jesus would have said if he had stepped into that conversation circle? Would he have given them a fresh reason to believe?

Hey, Journal,

I was right; Mama was so surprised to see me home a day early, she tripped over a planter as she flew out the door. "Are Papa and your brothers heading home, too?" she asked.

Uncle Lem aimed a quick wink in my direction. "No, Benjamin and I had business in town," he said. "I'll need to return to deliver supplies, but this young man's all done for now—aren't you, Benjamin?"

"Uh, yes ... I mean, sure. I helped mend nets yesterday because the wind was too strong to take the boat out to sea."

"Oh, that's too bad. I know how you were looking forward to fishing," said Mama. "Well, there'll be other opportunities to fish."

I followed Uncle Lem to the end of our street. "I'm not sure if I want to fish after all," I said. "I was thinking, maybe I could visit Timothy sometime."

Uncle Lem looked like I'd dumped cold water over his head. "Now why would you want to do that? You've barely given fishing a try, Benjamin. Timothy will try to turn you into a shepherd overnight. Besides, don't you have to return to your studies?"

My uncle would probably never admit it, but I think he's disappointed that Timothy chose the life of a shepherd. His tight-lipped expression shouted disapproval.

"Rabbi isn't expecting me back for another day," I explained. "It won't take me long to catch up."

"Speak to your mother," he said. "If she says it's alright, I'll head up to Timothy's hill with you. Hurry, though; I need to deliver these supplies before the sea wind decides to pick up again."

Mother's face brightened when I told her what I wanted to do. "Take a warm cloak," she said, "and here—I'll pack some food for you to share with Timothy this evening."

Uncle Lem led me up into the hilly area where his son kept a small herd of sheep. We spotted Timothy huddled next to a fire with his back to us. Uncle Lem gave me a signal to hush, and I watched him sneak up behind his son. "Grrrrrr-rrrrrrrrrr!" he snarled. "It's a hungry bear, hunting for a plump, juicy lamb."

"Very funny, Father," laughed Timothy. "Hey, Benjy! What brings you way out here?"

"It's Benjamin, and I've been wanting to visit you for the longest time. Today works fine for me if it's okay with you."

Timothy rubbed his hands together expectantly. "Great! Well, I hope you're braced for visitors in the wee hours of the night," he said in an exaggerated whisper. "You know, bears, jackals, and long-fanged wolves. Wild boar ... leopards ... hedgehogs."

Uncle Lem played along. "You did bring your slingshot, didn't you Benjamin?"

Those two were making me nervous. Maybe I didn't want to stay after all. Maybe I'm not cut out for living outdoors.

"Gotcha!" said Timothy. Father and son shared a good laugh at my expense.

"I need to get going, Benjamin, or your dad is going to send a search team out for us. He embraced us both, then whispered in my ear, "Watch your back. Those jackals are the worst! They'll sneak up behind a kid your size and before you know it, you're dinner."

"Thanks for the warning," I said in my bravest voice.

View from a Lean-To

Hey, Journal,

We watched Uncle Lem follow the trail back down the hill, toward the fishing camp. Timothy didn't turn away until his father had shrunk to the size of a dot. When at last he spoke, his melancholy tone grabbed my full attention. "My father," he began haltingly, "is not the easiest person to get along with. I love him dearly, but—" He stopped in mid-sentence, suddenly self-conscious.

"Timothy, what's wrong? Are you guys having problems?"

"No, we're fine," he said. "We hardly ever argue, but we don't talk much either—at least not about things that really matter." He took a long breath, like someone who has a lot on his mind. "Father and I are very different people," he explained. "He's a true-blue fisherman. I'm a dedicated shepherd. But the truth is, I'll never fish and he'll never tend sheep."

I didn't get it. "Well, what's wrong with that?"

Bonnie Bruno

"My father is big on tradition," said Timothy, "but hard as I try, I can't stand the thought of spending hours waiting for slimy fish to jump into a net. It's not what I want to do with the rest of my life."

"Me, neither," I said. "Papa is anxious for me to join his crew someday, but I don't have the heart to tell him how I really feel."

"You're only twelve, Benjamin," Timothy reminded me. "It's not like you have to decide anything tonight."

He was right. Why do I pressure myself so? "I don't want to hurt his feelings, but I know if I don't make up my mind, there'll be no way out. Papa will make up my mind for me, and I'll be stuck on that fishing crew for the rest of my life."

"Sounds horrible," groaned Timothy.

"Like a nightmare," I groaned back.

Timothy and I stuffed ourselves on fishcakes, rolls, and a mixture of fruit and nuts. We talked fast to make up for lost time. He's three years older than me, but age has never made much of a difference. We've practically grown up in each other's homes, and I feel more like his brother than his cousin. *Since he's taken over the flock, we only get to see each other every few months.*

"So, how are Abe and Micah doing?" Timothy asked between bites of dinner. "Have they fallen overboard yet?"

"Hardly!" I laughed. "None of us got to go near the water this time, thanks to the wild wind. We spent all of our time mending nets." I stifled a yawn. "Booooring."

Timothy kept one eye on his sheep while we ate. When one fuzzy little lamb strayed down the hill too far, he used his staff to gently prod it back to its mother. "That little fella is one of our wanderers," he said, patting its wooly back. "Fortunately, the older sheep usually know better."

The shepherd's life brings out the gentle side of a person. I can't picture some of the rough-tough fishermen on Papa's crew chasing after a lost lamb. My cousin seems happiest there on the hilltop, just as fishermen crave life on the sea. I envy Timothy, and I wish I were old enough to have my own flock. *Someday I will, God willing.* Silently I prayed that God would agree.

The last hour of daylight flickered across our faces. "Just wait till the sky lights up with stars," said Timothy. "You'll feel like you're at the very beginning of Creation."

Hey, Journal,

After the sheep settled down for the night, Timothy and I curled up inside a wooden lean-to, where we had a clear view of the flock. Moonlight splashed the ground in shiny yellow blotches, illuminating huge-bellied ewes who would soon give birth.

"The lambing season is the best time of year," said Timothy. "It's a lot of hard work, but there's nothing more exciting than seeing new life begin."

I unrolled a blanket and wrapped it around my shoulders. *This is the life for me!* I thought. Timothy was right about the stars. The skyful of glitter looked close enough to reach out and touch. Below our hill, the lamps of Bethsaida twinkled a friendly hello. I felt like a king overseeing his kingdom. (I doubt that a king would wrap himself in such a scratchy, smelly old wool blanket, though.)

Timothy guessed my thoughts. "If you stick around here long enough, you'll see that it's not all starry skies and fun-around-the-fire, Benjamin. Shepherding is not a job for the fainthearted. My blankets are old and scratchy, and there's usually nobody to talk to up here except for the sheep."

"Well, the good news is that sheep don't talk back," I said.

"True," agreed Timothy. "They do talk, though, in their own way. They tell me when they're hungry or when something's lurking out there in the dark."

He went on to describe a night when a wolf prowled the hillside. "I didn't dare close an eye, for fear he'd eat me alive," he said. "The sheep were huddled so tightly, I thought the little ones in the middle were going to be crushed."

That piece of news kept me awake for hours. I pulled my blanket up to my nose and lay as still as possible. Every few minutes, I'd lift my head to see how the sheep were behaving. They looked carefree and at peace, but this wannabe shepherd boy wasn't about to turn into anybody's midnight snack!

When at last I fell asleep, daybreak rudely interrupted it. I sat up in a groggy gray haze and couldn't remember where I was or how I got there. My clothes felt clammy, thanks to a heavy dew that had found its way into our shelter. I reached over to give Timothy a gentle shake, but his bedroll was empty. *Timothy's been mauled by a wild boar or eaten by a pack of wolves! Could he have fallen in a ravine while rescuing a sheep?*

"Over here," I heard Timothy call. He stood in a wide stripe of sunlight that stretched from one side of the hill to the other.

"I thought you'd been eaten," I said. "I was going to search for a little pile of bones to bury."

Timothy pulled his heavy cape close, to ward off the chill. "That's what I like about you. You always look on the bright side," he said sarcastically. He patted the ground next to him. "Stand here a few minutes to thaw out before you leave," he said.

44

My mouth flew open. "Who says I'm leaving?"

"Oh, I can tell," he said with a sly grin. "Almost all my visitors rush off after one night. They arrive thinking it's going to be all moonlight, stars, and cuddly sheep, and they leave happy to have made it out alive." I knew he was kidding, yet there was some truth in what he said.

After just two nights away, I was homesick and hungry. The fish fry with Papa's crew was nothing to brag about, and Timothy's meager dinner hardly filled me up, either.

"If you weren't in such a hurry, I'd heat you a cup of cinnamon tea," said Timothy. "Here, at least take a pastry with you."

"Thanks, Cousin," I said, accepting the sweet treat. "I think I'll eat on the run. If I make it home in time, I might surprise Rabbi and show up for class today."

Timothy kissed both my cheeks, as was the custom of close friends and family members. "Go in peace," he said, "but come back soon, okay? Maybe next time we can wrestle a bear or track down a wild boar for dinner."

"I'll be back," I called, and I really meant it.

Bonnie Bruno

Hilltop Hideaway

Hey, Journal,

I was glad for some time to think on the walk home. My head was bursting with memories of the past two days. I felt like I had been split in half—first a fisherman, and then a shepherd. I was exhausted, and home sounded like a welcome change.

"Benjamin! Benjamin, look up here, at the top of the hill!" I heard Peter yell.

A quick survey of the hill turned up nothing but bushes, boulders, and tall grass bending in the breeze.

"Benjamin, up here, to your left!"

Peter stood on a boulder waving both arms. What in the world was he doing running around the hill country so early in the morning?

We met halfway up the hill. "Are you nuts?" I asked him. "What are you doing all the way out here by yourself at this hour?"

"I could ask you the same thing," said Peter. "Have you lost your mind? Well, maybe I should rephrase that. Have you lost what's left of your mind?"

"Very funny. Who made you a comedian?"

Peter waved his arm dramatically, like someone leading a tour. "This is my domain," he said dramatically. "Come on, I'll show you around."

"I don't have time," I protested. "Believe it or not, I'm trying to get home so I can get ready for school. I've been out fishing with my father. Well, sort of."

Peter held his nose. "That explains the smell," he said, rolling his eyes.

My clothes smelled dirty from sleeping near the sheep pen, but that was another story. I didn't need Peter blabbing my business in class, so I skipped the part about helping Timothy.

Peter motioned for me to follow. "You're going to love this," he said.

I trailed him to the top of the hill, to a clump of bushes. Behind the bushes sat a huge curved rock formation. "Hold your applause," said Peter. "You haven't seen anything yet."

He parted two bushes in front, then crawled under a raggedy cloth that hung from a branch overhead. "Welcome to my hideaway," he said, stepping inside.

"A fort!" I cried. "And look—you even have fresh air and light." Tiny holes in the ceiling let in streams of light and fresh air.

No wonder Peter was such a genius! If I had a hilltop hideaway like that, I'd be a whiz kid, too. The cave was quiet and peaceful, a perfect place to study. "How'd you discover this cave?"

Peter jammed his hands in the pockets of his robe. "It wasn't hard. I bet these hills have dozens of caves just like this."

Peter offered me a cool drink. He popped open the lid to a wooden bin and pulled out an apple. "Want a snack?" The place was fully furnished and would make a great place to land after school every day. Maybe he'll invite me back sometime soon.

I would have gladly stayed there all day, but I had to get home if I was going to make it to class on time. Mama was probably pacing by now. You'd think she'd be used to my side-tracked ways, but she claims it's a mother's right to worry.

I reached home in time to eat a few bites of breakfast before school. Lydia flew around the corner to greet me and bombarded me with one question after another. "How many fish did you catch, Benjy? Did you get seasick? Did the storm toss the boat around?" I thought she'd never shut up.

"No, I didn't get seasick, and no, I didn't catch fish."

She looked like someone had knocked the wind out of her. "Huh? No fish? Why not?"

She gave it some thought, then started over. "How many fishes did you catch, Benjy—*really?*"

"Zero," I said, circling my index finger and thumb into a big fat O.

"No, I mean it!" argued Lydia. "How many fishes did you catch?"

I held my hand up again. "Zero, Lydia. None. Absolutely, positively none. In fact, I didn't even *see* a fish the whole time I was there. The closest I got to the water was when the wind blew mist across my face. The water was too choppy," I explained, "so we had to take care of boring chores like mending nets."

Bonnie Bruno

Lydia made a face. "I don't ever want to be a boy. Not ever!"

"Relax, Lydia. That's one thing you don't have to worry about, I promise."

Mama poured water into a washing bowl. "Go ahead—it's yours if you'd like," said Mama. "Lydia and I can freshen up later."

I carried the bowl of hot water to my room, where I scrubbed away layers of grit and grime. Rabbi had excused me to go fishing with my papa; I didn't dare show up at school smelling like a sheep pen!

At breakfast, I mentioned Peter's cave to Mama.

"A fort! It sounds like every boy's dream," she said.

"He has so much stuff in it, it almost feels like a house," I said enviously. "And guess what? He said there are dozens more caves like his up in the hills."

"Well, don't get any ideas, Benjy. Most of them already have occupants—the four-legged kind." The thought made me shudder. Would a snarly beast of the hills return to reclaim Peter's cave someday?

The walk to school gave me more time to think. I'd only been away two days, yet it felt like weeks. I'd sampled a day in the life of a fisherman and come away disappointed. In fact, I doubted I would ever use the words "fun" and "fish" in the same sentence again. My night on the hillside with Timothy wasn't that memorable, either.

I thought of Timothy's advice. Maybe I do need to slow down and focus on one thing at a time. Today, that meant focusing on schoolwork.

Rabbi's plump face stretched into a grin when I marched into class. "Welcome back," he called. "I'm happy to see that our storm the other night didn't pick you up and carry you off. So, how was the fishing?"

"Great!" I said. I could feel a fish story coming on—a very big fish story. What would my friends think of me if I told them the truth—that I didn't even go near the water?

Everyone waited. The pressure was on. Who was I to disappoint them?

"I don't want to cut into your lesson time, Rabbi, Sir, but I will say this: By the end of the day, I was so exhausted, I curled up in my father's boat and fell asleep," I said. "That's where I woke up in the morning."

Let them reach their own conclusions, I figured.

Rabbi patted me on the back. "Wonderful, wonderful. We will look forward to hearing more about your trip some other time. Now, let's begin today's lesson, shall we?"

Rabbi must have taken pity on me, because he didn't call on me to recite—not even once. Tomorrow I would be prepared—a promise I made myself during my walk home. School will buy me enough time to decide what I want to do with the rest of my life. It's a big decision and every time I ponder it, my brain ends up in knots.

After class, Peter took off without me. "So, how did your fishing trip go—really?" he asked. He eyed me suspiciously like a doctor probing for a clue to an illness.

"Great. Well, not great, but good enough."

"And what, exactly, is 'good enough'?" said Peter. He slapped his hand over his mouth to hide a smirk.

"I learned a lot, alright?" Peter was getting on my nerves fast. "My father invited me to taste the life of a fisherman, but the best part was staying with my cousin, who's a shepherd. A night on the hill is no place for weaklings, Peter. The country-side is crawling with wild beasts that only come out after dark."

"Woo-hoo!" shouted Peter. "You must've gotten quite an education out in the smelly pasture, dodging sheep pies."

Peter's lucky I was in a good mood. He doesn't know how close I came to punching him. "Well, it's obvious you don't know anything about shepherding," I said. I explained a typical day in the life of a shepherd. "It's not all starry skies and sit-around-the-fire, Peter."

Peter wasn't listening. His eyes had locked on a white-robed stranger who stood far off the road, in the center of a bustling crowd. Grabbing both my shoulders, Peter asked, "Benjamin, come up for air! Look—Do you have any idea who that is?"

A Stranger in Town

Peter pushed his way into the crowd. Onlookers held their ground and refused to budge. "Imagine having that kind of following," said Peter, shaking his head. "He must feel like royalty."

Suddenly a woman's voice cried out, "Jesus! Jesus!"

Jesus? Here in Bethsaida? My jaw dropped. "Peter, what's he doing here? I heard he was in Capernaum, not Bethsaida."

"Well, it's not like he announces a traveling schedule," said Peter. "I've heard that he has been traveling all around the area close to the Sea of Galilee. He and twelve men—*disciples,* they call them—wander from place to place. You never know where he'll turn up next."

"Who told you all that? Your parents?"

Peter jerked away and ignored my question. Every time I bring up his parents or siblings, he freezes. End of conversation. It's just plain weird, if you ask me.

A young man elbowed my ribs as he pushed his way out of the tight throng. He wore the expression of someone who had received the shock of his life. "How did he know my name?

I've never met him before, yet he knew everything about me!"

"Sir, are you alright?" I asked.

"Better than I've ever been!" he exclaimed. "I was lost—invisible to everyone around me! Now I feel whole. *Whole!*" He shook his head and brushed a wisp of flyaway hair away from his brow. "I was lost and he found me! Surely this is no ordinary man!"

Peter grabbed my arm. "Did you hear that? That guy has to be Jesus. He's the only one I've ever heard of who can pull off a trick like that."

If I had been a mouse, I would have scampered right between all those ankles to the very front. I would have sat at Jesus' feet and watched his every move. As word spread, people rushed forward—hot sweaty bodies pushing and elbowing each other for a better look.

I couldn't take it anymore. "If we don't get out of here, we're going to be crushed!" I cried.

Peter and a middle-aged gentleman were chattering so fast, they sounded like two squirrels. "Haven't you heard?" said Peter. "Jesus has a bag of tricks bigger than Bethsaida. Nobody can figure him out, but some people say that he is the Son of God."

The crowd was growing more restless by the minute. "What's all the fuss about?" said one lady, craning her neck to get a glimpse of Jesus. "He's a showman, that's all, just your everyday showman."

A widow dressed in black whipped around, wagging her finger at the younger woman. "Watch your tongue there, Missy! You don't know what you're talking about. With my own two eyes, I saw him heal a lame man! My eyes don't lie, but your tongue is spewing venom!"

"Benjamin, look, he's leaving!" shouted Peter. "Jesus is leaving."

A mother with two wiggly young children worked her way out of the congregation. "This is nuts," she said. "You people are all hysterical. Jesus is impressive, but he's just an ordinary person like the rest of us, not a god."

I wanted to ask how an "ordinary person" could perform miracles like the ones I'd heard about. Word has it that Jesus healed a woman who had suffered with a lifelong illness, too.

Peter stood atop a boulder to watch the crowd break up. Jesus and his friends had wandered off in the opposite direction. I wonder if he ever tires of all those crowds? Everywhere he goes, a crowd gathers. The scene reminded me of the way Lydia is always jumping around trying to get my attention. "Everyone wants something from him," I said, shaking my head.

Someday I would like to meet Jesus face-to-face. I wonder what he would say to me. Would he ask my name or know it already? Would he tell me things about myself that only my parents could know? Seems kind of spooky!

Hey, Journal,

The first eleven years of my life, I could hardly wait to be twelve. Well, I've been twelve for almost a year now and nothing is really all that different. Mama still gets upset when I arrive home late. Papa still wonders if all of his father-to-son talks will pay off. And I have a hunch that they both ponder whether I'll ever grow into a responsible young adult like Abe and Micah.

Most of all, I think Papa wonders if I'll step into what he

calls my "rightful place" as a fisherman. After the lost-needle fiasco, he probably isn't wondering about that anymore! I don't think he'll ever invite me back, especially since I broke his number-one rule and left without permission. Nobody walks away from his fishing crew, no matter what. If someone was bleeding to death, they'd have to ask his permission to leave.

If I hadn't left early, though, I would have missed my appointment with Jesus! Nothing happens by accident. Everything takes place in its own time, and today was my day to see this man who is healing bodies and changing lives.

What about the man whose life was changed by such an appointment? He said he felt lost until Jesus found him. He said meeting Jesus was like receiving a new life even though he's grown up. What a mysterious, wondrous gift!

Dusk was caressing the field where Jesus stood just moments ago.

"I need to hurry," I told Peter. "My mom's probably having a fit about now, wondering where I am."

Why does he always turn away whenever I mention either of my parents? "Same here," he answered quietly.

"Hey, Peter? I've been wondering something. What kind of work does your father do? Is he a fisherman like Papa, or what?"

"Yeah, more or less." He picked up the pace and kept on walking. "I gotta speed it up or I'll be late, Benjamin."

"See you tomorrow at school?" I asked, but he ignored my question.

We parted at our usual spot. "Hey!" I called after him. "Where do you live, anyway?"

Peter pointed to a row of hills. "Over there," he replied,

without looking back. "Way over there."

Way over *where?* The only thing between here and there are hills, farmers' fields, and the sea.

If I hurried, I'd arrive at my house on the corner before Mama noticed how late it is. When God made mothers, he must have given them a list of worries. My mother is forever worrying about things like wild animals, robbers, and bad weather. And if those aren't enough, she worries about whether I'm eating enough, sleeping enough, and studying enough.

One time I joked about my mother to Peter. "Just be glad she worries," he snapped. "Just be glad she's there, *period.*" Peter is a good friend, yet he sometimes speaks a different language. All I really know about him is what he lets me see at school. Sometimes he seems as lost as the man who met Jesus today.

I wonder, if Jesus had come closer today, would Peter have reached down to touch the hem of his garment, too?

Bonnie Bruno

What's Wrong with Peter?

Hey, Journal,

My feet felt like blocks of wood when I left for school this morning. School is so much work! I always dread the thought of Rabbi's piercing stare. Before he calls on anyone, he studies each face, as if he can tell whether we studied. The truth is, I only spent a few minutes on homework last night. How could anyone study after witnessing what I saw on the outskirts of town yesterday?

Mama thinks I worry too much. Just relax, she says, and things will work out fine. (Why doesn't she take her own advice?) Papa thinks I need to take school more seriously. He suggests that I practice my daily lessons by reciting each Scripture passage to the bedroom wall. (Parents have the strangest ideas!)

The closer I got to the synagogue, the more I dragged my feet. I thought of Timothy, whose hilltop pasture felt like another world. Now that I'd had time to settle back into my usual routine, I missed my adventure with my cousin. What a view! What a great job! Timothy is faithful to his task because he is excited about his work. That's the kind of job I hope to have someday—work that feels like a perfect fit. I wonder if God already knows what I will become? Does he have something special in mind for me? I sure hope it won't include mending nets on a windy beach.

Hey, Journal,

What a crazy day! I showed up this morning on time for school, but nobody was around. The shady spot under the huge old tree was empty. I didn't see any lunch-baskets or cloaks—nothing. *Maybe Rabbi took everyone on one of his rollicking field trips to the marketplace.*

"Are you lost, young man?" called a familiar voice. It was Jacob, the groundskeeper at the synagogue. His leathery face is lined with wrinkles—"character tracks," he calls them. I agree; Jacob is quite a character!

"I'm not lost, but where's everyone else?" I asked.

Jacob pursed his lips and tried to look serious. "The information will cost you."

"Well, to tell you the truth, I don't care whether I find them or not. I'd just as soon go home—or head back to help my cousin tend sheep. School exhausts me!"

Jacob loves working outdoors. I thought he'd surely agree with me, but he was no help at all! He pointed to a window across the sunny courtyard. "Sorry, friend. I'd love to send you on your merry way, but Rabbi would string me up by my ankles if I did that." He laughed at his own comment. "Now don't just stand there, get moving," he said. "Your classmates are waiting

60

for your grand arrival. They're meeting in the room overlooking the garden."

I kicked a rock across the wide garden courtyard. Rabbi was going to make a big issue out of my tardiness. I'd have to sneak into class when he wasn't looking. My plan was foiled, though, when an obnoxious classmate spotted me tiptoeing in. "Well looky there, it's Benjamin-the-Tardy! Where ya been?"

I dropped to a spot on the mat next to him and threw him my best glare. "Why don't you just announce it to the whole world!"

Rabbi stepped around the circle of boys and stopped directly in front of me. His robe smelled like last night's onions. "Well, look who has decided to join us. Just in time for your recitation, too," said Rabbi. The boy nearest the door wiggled his eyebrows several times to try to make me laugh. "Are you prepared, Benjamin?"

Peter gasped when I stood to face the class. If I hadn't been so nervous, I would have laughed at his reaction. His whole face tensed up, as if he was about to witness an execution or something.

I took a deep breath and began. "Okay, this is from the eighteenth psalm of David: 'I love you, Lord. You give me strength. The Lord is my rock and my fort. He is the One who saves me. He is like a shield to me. He's the power that saves me. He's my place of safety.'"

The whole class broke into spontaneous applause. The obnoxious kid whistled between his teeth and stomped his feet. Rabbi didn't make an effort to hush my classmates. "Take a bow, Benjamin," he said, patting me on the back. "A well-earned bow, at that!"

I tore out the door after class, with Peter sprinting close behind. "What was *that?*" he said. "I've never heard such a smooth delivery."

"Why, are you jealous?" I kidded him. Peter looked like a king who'd been dethroned.

"Of course not. I've just never heard you recite that well before." Peter changed the subject. "So, did you get in trouble when you got home late yesterday?" he asked.

"Nope. How about you?"

"Nope. My parents don't care one way or the other."

I cast a sideways look at Peter. "Oh, so your parents don't mind you wandering around after dark?"

"Like I said, everything's fine," said Peter. "It's not like I'm eight or nine. I'm thirteen and they trust me. Your mom must be a lot stricter than mine."

Peter could talk big, but I knew better. Every parent I know would be worried (not to mention angry) if their child was out past dark. I'd like to meet any parent who thinks it's "fine." "Hey, Peter," I said, "I've been wondering. When will I get to meet your family?"

"Sometime soon," he promised.

"Well, how about coming to my house tomorrow night for dinner? You can meet my family first, and then I can meet yours. Deal?"

Peter drew back. "By the time I get home and do my homework and chores, it's almost time for bed. Then I get up and start all over again. It's not like we live three doors away from you, Benjamin."

"Peter, you're much too serious," I said, slapping him on the back. "Lighten up. It'll lengthen your life."

"Oh, do the Scriptures say that?" said Peter. "I think you're mixed up. I recall the Scriptures saying that God promises a long life to those who honor their parents."

I can always count on Peter-the-Brilliant to put me in my place. He's a Scripture whiz, a walking, talking Rabbi-in-training. I wonder if he inherited his sharp mind and quick memory from his parents.

"So who did you inherit your good memory from—your mother or father?" I asked.

Peter shrugged. "Both." We'd reached the end of the road. "Here's my turnoff," he said. "See you tomorrow."

"Peter, wait! I was wondering—"

My mysterious friend kept walking and didn't look back.

Hey, Journal,

Papa returned from the sea today after a successful two days of fishing. He was the picture of fatigue—bloodshot eyes, and drooping shoulders. "I ache from head to toe," he said, then added, "Are you sure you want to be a fisherman, Benjamin?"

Oh, how I wanted to shout, "Not at all, Papa. I want to be a shepherd—at least I think I do." Instead, I kept quiet and kneaded his tight shoulder muscles. "You should have heard me today," I said. "Rabbi looked like he was witnessing a miracle or something."

"I'm proud of you, son," said Papa. He gave my arm a squeeze. "That's what I like to hear. It sounds like you're headed in the right direction."

"I took your advice. I've been talking to my wall every night. Peter thinks I'm nuts, but hey, it works for me."

I described Peter's shifty ways to Papa. "I've never had a

friend quite like him. Sometimes he acts as if he wants to tell me something, but then he loses his nerve. The only place Peter seems totally relaxed is at his hilltop hideaway.

Papa looked puzzled. "Hilltop hideaway? Where?"

"Oh, not far from where Timothy tends his sheep. Peter calls it a fort, but it's really a cave," I explained.

Mama looked concerned. "Benjamin, do you think Peter might actually live there in the cave?"

"Impossible," I said, rolling the thought over in my head. "How could someone his age live all alone? Where would he eat? How would he stay warm on cold nights. Where would he wash his clothes or take a bath?"

Papa shook his head and sighed. "Wild animals live in some of the hill caves, Benjamin. I hope Peter is cautious. It could be bad news if a wild boar or wolf returns home and finds him living there."

"I guarantee, this cave is fit for a king, Papa. A boar wouldn't feel at home in that fancy fort."

Mama was not going to give up. "Well, it's not safe! What are his parents thinking, anyway?"

"I have no idea. Every time I ask about his parents, he changes the subject."

It's true. I've lost track of the times I've been snubbed by Peter after asking about his family. Something is wrong with him, and sooner or later I'm going to solve the mystery. Peter's secret life is turning into the missing piece of our friendship.

Friend or Foe?

Hey, Journal,

Something strange thing happened on the way to school today. I passed Peter, who was hurrying in the opposite direction.

"Hey, where are you headed?" I asked, turning to catch up with him. "You look like an animal on a hunt."

"I can't talk," Peter said breathlessly. "I'll see you later at school."

"Wait! Can I go with you?" I asked, but Peter was insistent.

"No! I said I'll see you at school."

I waited outside our classroom until Rabbi finally herded us inside, but Peter never showed up. During recess, I made a decision. Didn't the Scriptures speak about the importance of being a loyal friend? My friend must be in some kind of trouble. How could I turn my back on him in his hour of need? I decided to investigate.

I was pretty sure I knew where he might have gone, and if my hunch was right, I could be there in a few minutes. First, I

Bonnie Bruno

stopped by the house. The last thing I needed was for my parents to hear that I'd left school early. I was not surprised when Mama gave me her blessing. "Would you like me to go with you?" she offered.

"No, I need to do this myself," I said. "Peter's on the shy side. I don't want to scare him off."

"Well, at least let me make you boys a lunch," said Mama. She gathered some bread twists, dried fruit, and a delicious fish spread she'd concocted from leftovers. "Oh, and Benjamin," she added, "tell Peter that his family is welcome to join us for dinner sometime soon. Tomorrow or the next day would be fine."

Our family is far from wealthy, but Mama always loves to share whatever we have. "God allows some of us to barely scrape out a living in order to teach us how to trust. And when you trust, he'll never let you down, Peter."

Mama has a knack for sharing nuggets of wisdom in ordinary, everyday situations. She has an answer for everything. When I lost an argument with a neighborhood buddy, for example, she said, "Friends will come and go, but God is as steady as the seasons."

Hey, Journal,

Rain dampened my face on the way to Peter's hilltop hideaway. I thought about my mother's words: *God is as steady as the seasons.* I wonder, has Peter ever learned to trust God?

I reached the grassy hill in record time, just as sunshine broke through the clouds. Steam rose like a morning prayer during my hike to the top. If my hunch was right, Peter had run here to his hideaway. I suppose everyone needs a hideaway of some kind or another. Mine is a grassy knoll that overlooks the sea. I go there occasionally when I crave silence. Hopefully, that's what Peter has done this morning—hurried here in search of peace and quiet. And hopefully, he won't be mad at me for following him.

The bushes near the entrance to Peter's hideaway waved their branches in a breezy hello. Was Peter tucked away inside the cave? Would he answer my call or pretend he wasn't there?

"Peter! Hey, Peter!" I cried. I parted the bushes and stepped up to the entrance. "Peter, it's Benjamin. Can I come in?"

The only answer came from the wind. Something must be terribly wrong. What if he'd found a wild wolf rummaging through his things? What if he was too weak to answer and needed my help? I had no choice but to rescue him, so I jerked open the raggedy covering hanging over the entrance to the cave.

I heard a raspy noise. Was it the sound of breathing? "Peter?" I called softly. "Pssst! Hey, Peter!"

Peter had added more furnishings since my first visit. A bed hugged one wall, next to a container filled with clothes. My snoopy side took over and I peeked inside a small bin. The deep wooden container was filled with food—lots of it! Dried fruit ... nuts ... and something that looked like strips of dried fish or jerky.

A damp, stale odor hung in the air like sickening incense. It reminded me of how a dry creek bed smells a few minutes after a downpour. I checked out every corner, like a dog sniffing for food. As far as I could tell, Peter hadn't been there recently.

My imagination took over, as usual. *What if a jackal or a bear had attacked and turned his meaty frame into their morning meal?* A wet puddle near the entrance caught my attention. Blood? My heart beat double-time as I dipped a finger in it. Whew! It was only water—probably rainwater dripping from a pinhole crack on the cave's ceiling.

As the minutes wore on, I realized that Peter must have been hurrying somewhere else. Maybe he'd forgotten his lunch and was rushing home to get it. Had I worried all day for nothing? I imagined him back at school, wondering why I hadn't shown up for class. He was probably sitting in his usual spot up front, reciting the Scripture reading at that very moment, much to Rabbi's delight.

I felt suddenly out of place, like a burglar sorting through a stranger's belongings.

"I gotta get out of here," I said aloud.

A voice blurted out, "So, did you find what you're looking for?" Peter stood in the entrance, glaring at me. "What do you think you're doing, Benjamin?" he roared. "Who do you think you are, barging into my house?"

His house? Did I really hear him say that? The fort was comfortable, but how could anybody actually live in that mildew-infested place? "Sorry, Peter," I said, trying to make amends. "When you passed me this morning, I thought sure you were in some kind of trouble. You should know by now that I'm not the kind of friend who walks away from trouble. If a friend needs help, I'm there."

Peter wasn't convinced. "So are you saying that you wouldn't be upset if you found me rummaging through your stuff? Hmmm? What right do you have to force your way in here like you own the place?"

Peter was right. What business did I have there, snooping

through his stuff? I hung my head, like a thief who had gotten caught. "Sorry," I said softly. "I was just worried about you, that's all. You've been acting odd lately, and then this morning you rushed by and—"

"Well, mind your own business from now on!" screamed Peter. "There's nothing to worry about, okay? I can take care of myself. Got that?"

I shoved Mama's basketful of food at Peter, but neither of us had much of an appetite. "Here. Eat it for dinner tonight."

An unspoken question hung between us like a fog bank. When I couldn't stand the silence, I spoke up. "Peter, sooner or later, I want to talk," I said. "If you want my help, please remember that I'm here for you."

Peter's eyes clouded with tears. "I just can't talk about it, okay?" he said. "At least not today. Please don't ask me again, Benjamin. If we're going to be friends, you've got to know something up front."

Peter stared at me with a faraway expression. Was this the same smart kid who acted so calm and controlled in class? "I'm all ears," I said.

"Oh, what's the use?" he groaned. "Do me a favor, will you, Benjamin? Get out and don't come back unless you're invited."

Part of me stung from his words, but the other part ached from wanting to help my friend. I had a dilemma: How could I help someone who wouldn't admit that he has a problem? *Dear God,* I prayed, *"I don't know what to do. Please show me how to help Peter.*

I knew in my heart that Peter wasn't ready to receive help; it was pointless to keep trying. I also knew that God was the only one who could fix whatever was troubling him. "Suit yourself,"

I said quietly. "But don't expect me to stay away for long, Peter. Something is wrong and I'm not giving up. A friend doesn't desert a friend in need!"

At that moment, Peter felt more like a stranger than the friend who scrambled up the rock with me to steal a glimpse of Jesus just a couple of days ago.

"Should I let Rabbi know that you won't be at school tomorrow?" I asked.

Peter pulled the door covering aside and gestured for me to leave. "How about minding your own business for once, Benjamin? Let me worry about when I'll return to school."

His words stung like a hard slap. I left without giving him the satisfaction of a reply. The wet, slippery grass knocked me off balance, and I slid halfway down the grassy slope. Normally, I would have picked myself up and laughed hysterically, but not today. I glanced up at the hilltop to see if he was watching me leave. Peter was gone.

Like a
Lost Lamb

Hey, Journal,

I'd walked a short way when I heard someone calling my name. "Benjamin! Up here!"

Imagine my surprise when I discovered Cousin Timothy perched atop a nearby hill, waving both arms. What was he doing so far from his usual pasture? I cupped my hands and called up to him, "Give me a second and I'll join you."

"What's up, anyway?" I asked. "What brings you over this way?"

"Three of my best lambs decided to run off this afternoon. If can find at least one of them, the others will follow. Sheep are followers, you know."

"Wait right here. I know someone who might be able to help." I scrambled back up the hill and called out to Peter. I wouldn't blame him if he ignored my pleas. In fact, I wouldn't blame him if he never spoke to me again.

"Peter, I need your help," I shouted. "Please?"

Bonnie Bruno

Peter didn't waste time poking his head out. "What do you want?" he said gruffly. "I don't remember inviting you back."

"My cousin lost three of his best lambs. He needs to find them before dusk, or they'll be eaten alive by a wild animal."

"Spare me your melodrama, Benjamin," said Peter. "Just tell me what you want, okay?"

Here we go. I can already hear his no. "Well, I was hoping you'd help me and Timothy search for three runaway lambs. And Peter, I'm really sorry—"

Peter's reaction surprised me. "Forget it, Benjamin. You already apologized, remember? Just give me a minute to grab some sandals, and I'll catch up with you, okay?"

I found Timothy on the opposite hill, searching along a row of bushes that led into a narrow gully. "Sometimes lambs follow the vegetation line and end up stuck in the pricker bushes. Or, if they fall and end up lodged in a chasm, they either starve to death or are easy prey for hungry predators.

Timothy's expression brightened as soon as he saw us. "Hey, Peter! How goes it? I haven't seen you in ages."

"You two know each other?" I asked.

"Yep. Peter and I are practically neighbors," explained Timothy. "He's helped me round up more than a few runaways, too."

"So, do you know which direction your lambs headed?" asked Peter.

"I think they might have strayed toward the Jordan River. A few of their wooly friends graze the fields there, and they might have gone for a visit."

Peter and Timothy tramped on ahead of me, tossing around shepherding terms that made me feel like an outsider. *How does Peter know so much about sheep, anyway?*

When we crested the next grassy hill, Peter cried out, "Check out this view! You can see forever from up here!" He looked toward a grassy field off in the distance. A dilapidated animal pen stretched across a corner of the field and was sheltered by a grove of shade trees.

"Look familiar?" I asked him.

Peter couldn't take his eyes off the field. In a voice choked with emotion, he replied, "Yes, it's where my father used to work."

I wish I could have crawled into his mind to read it. *There he goes, talking in code again.* Peter sometimes acts like he can't bring himself to trust anyone. I thought of the woman back in Bethsaida who reached down to touch the hem of Jesus' garment. Jesus knew exactly what was troubling her that day. He knew how to fix her inside and out—both her physical and spiritual problems. But the woman had to take an important step; she had to reach out and trust. I wonder, would Peter have taken that step?

Hey, Journal,

Timothy noticed Peter's quiet mood. "Listen, I have a question for you," he said. "I could use an extra pair of eyes and feet for the next few days. It's lambing season, and my ewes are threatening to have their babies all in the same week."

"So, do you need a midwife or a lamb-sitter?" joked Peter.

"Both," said Timothy.

"You'd better think before you say yes," I warned Peter. "My cousin here doesn't allow any slacking off. He has a reputation to preserve. Right, Timothy?"

As soon as the words left my mouth, I regretted my comment. What right did I have to butt into Timothy and Peter's business? Why do I always speak before I think?

"Relax, Benjamin," said Peter, tossing me a dirty look. "I can handle it.

"Here's a bright idea: Why don't you spend more time doing your homework, and I'll worry about the sheep. Sound like a good deal?"

From that point on, I might as well have been a rock or a tree. Peter and Timothy bantered back and forth as if I wasn't even there. I followed them around like an invisible moron tramping behind two longtime friends.

"How soon will you need help?" Peter asked my cousin.

"First thing tomorrow would work for me," said Timothy.

Peter beamed. "Sounds perfect! I'll be there."

Why doesn't Timothy ask me to help, too? After all, I'm family and Peter's not!

I wanted Peter to know that I had shepherding experience, too. "Hey, Timothy, remember the time I fell in the ravine between those two hills? I hollered until I was hoarse, and I thought you'd never come to my rescue."

"How could I forget?" said Timothy. He socked my arm and added, "You were the most stubborn excuse for a shepherd back then. Nobody runs around these hills on a pitch-black night except hungry predators or rebellious sheep."

I should have kept my mouth shut. Now I could add "ignorant" to my list of character traits. I was feeling dumber by the minute. *No use sticking around for more humiliation,* I figured. "I need to head home," I said.

"Not me," said Peter. "I'm going to hang in here until we find those lambs. If I were in their shoes ... hooves ... I'd sure want to be found, wouldn't you?"

Peter's question opened a window into his heart. Does he feel like a lost lamb, waiting to be found? I thought about pulling Timothy aside and filling him in on my friend's mysterious ways. Does he know Peter—the *real* Peter—as well as he thinks he does? Is he aware of Peter's secret hideaway up on the hill?

A still, quiet voice inside my head silenced me. *Let me work out the details,* God seemed to say. The older I get, the more I learn to recognize God's voice—when I choose to listen. Most of the time I'm too busy running my mouth or dreaming up my own schemes, though. When God speaks, he whispers words so clear and sure, I know they they could only come from him. This was such a moment.

Hey, Journal,

My walk home felt twice as long as usual.

"How's Peter doing?" asked Mama.

I didn't feel like discussing Peter's problems. "Oh, he's fine, I guess."

She studied my face the way mothers do and asked what was bothering me.

Mama has a flair for peering into my head. "I don't think Peter has a family," I whispered. My throat tightened around the next sentence. "I think he lives by himself in that so-called fort on the hill."

Mama wouldn't hear of it. "Oh, that's ridiculous, Benjamin. Everyone has a family somewhere. Do you suppose Peter is in some kind of trouble? Do you think he might have run away

Bonnie Bruno

from home? His family must be worried sick about him!"

"I don't think he's in trouble," I insisted. "But I do believe he lives alone."

"At twelve years old?" She shook her head in disbelief. "A boy his age can't survive on his own. How does he meet his basic needs like food and clothing? Surely he has grandparents or aunts and uncles who would take him in? And what about brothers or sisters?"

The more I thought about it, the crazier it sounded. Peter *has* to have somebody out there who cares about him—doesn't he? Isn't anybody missing him this very minute? Who does he celebrate special occasions with? Who does he run to when he has a problem?

"Peter's the smartest kid in class," I said, "but anybody who would choose to live in a dirty, drafty cave needs his head examined for holes."

I'm confused about how to help Peter. He's like one of Timothy's lost lambs, trying to find his way back. If I saw a lamb wandering close to a deep gully, would I just stand there? Of course not! I'd rush over and snatch him out of danger. Peter needs someone to find him—to discover the truth and lead him back. Lord, please show me how to help my friend.

Like a Lost Lamb

Papa's Confession

Hey, Journal,

I woke up thinking, *This is going to be a good day!* I'd worked hard on homework lately, and Rabbi has already promoted me to his list of top students. As a reward, my parents have agreed to let me spend a couple of days back on the hill, helping Timothy. Rabbi has given me his blessing, as long as I don't fall behind in my schoolwork.

Uncle Lem told Papa that Timothy's flock now boasts over a dozen new lambs. I can't wait to see them! I'm also anxious to ask Timothy about his time with Peter. Maybe he knows why Peter's so secretive.

Papa and I discussed Peter last night. "Don't worry, Benjamin," he said. "Peter probably just needs a quiet place to escape to now and then. Besides, what kid wouldn't like a fort of his own?"

I hope Papa is right. Maybe Peter's hilltop cave is just a place to relax every now and then. Maybe he has a home and a family who love him like crazy. Yes, I must talk to Timothy. Maybe he'll be able to put my mind at ease.

The higher I trekked up the winding trail up to Timothy's pasture, the more I heard the persistent bleating of newborn lambs. It sounded like a party going on—a very noisy, crowded party.

"Hey, long-lost cousin!" Timothy yelled down to me. "Come join the celebration!"

He met me halfway down the trail with big news. "Four of my best ewes gave birth last night!" he exclaimed. "Our 'family' has grown by fifteen members since you were here last, Benjamin."

"Ahhh-hh, it must be nice to have so many new brothers and sisters," I joked.

"And that's not the only good news," said Timothy. "I found all three lambs that were missing that day, thanks to Peter. He has a keen eye for this hilly area."

Two of the lambs had gotten wedged into a crevice. The third had run off and kept on running until its leg caught in a stickery hedge.

"Maybe Peter can relate to runaways," I said. I hoped that Timothy would pick up on my hint, but he ignored my comment.

I detected movement out of the corner of my eye. "Speaking of runaways, look there!" I shouted.

A fat ewe was inching her way toward the hillside. "Lois!" called Timothy. "Get back here!" The ewe stopped and turned. "She's probably looking for a cozy place to give birth. These mamas-to-be like to wander off a few hours before the big event."

Lois stopped in her tracks and stared vacantly at Timothy.

"Wow! She knows her name?" I asked.

"Of course. They all do," said Timothy.

I tried talking to the ewe, but she looked away. But when Timothy called to her again, she turned back.

"See, Benjamin? Sheep respond to their shepherd's voice," said Timothy. "It's another reason why I love it out here. They trust me completely."

I never miss an opportunity to poke fun at my cousin. "Ahhh, how sweet. You're like their daddy."

Lois meandered off in a different direction this time. "A shepherd gets a lot of exercise," laughed Timothy. "Some days it seems like all I do is chase down runaways. That's why I was so relieved to bump into Peter that day. I keep telling him that if he'll give me a week, I'll turn him into a real shepherd."

Timothy means it, too. He sized me up and added, "And you know the same invitation is open to you, Cousin. Anytime."

Timothy never says things just to flatter a person, so I took that as a true compliment. "Thanks, Cousin," I shot back. "As a matter of fact, I was hoping to stay and help you for a couple of days this week."

"Great!" cried Timothy. "You couldn't have chosen a more perfect time. Newborn lambs grow fast, and that's when things really start to hop around here. Look over there," he said, pointing to a lamb frolicking nearby. "See how much energy it has? She thinks the grownup sheep around here are boring. If I turn away too long, she'll be down the hill, galloping towards Bethsaida within minutes."

Our conversation ended abruptly at the sound of someone approaching. Papa!

My father huffed and puffed to the top of the hill. So surprised was I to see him, I asked, "Have you been following me?"

Papa gathered me in a sweaty hug. "Yes, I trailed you all the way from home, Benjamin, thinking, *Now, there's a kid who looks like a future fisherman!*"

I held back a groan. If only he knew what's been going on in my head lately, he'd realize how uninterested I am in the whole fishing scene. The grassy incense of this hillside tugged at me like a giant hook. I wonder what Papa would say if he knew the truth: If I had to choose today, I would not choose the life of a fisherman.

"So, Uncle Mark," called Timothy, "what brings you up here?"

"I'm heading home for the day," said Papa. "We caught so many fish last night, the merchants in town asked us to slow down. God blessed us with a huge catch. Fish were leaping into the boat, begging us to take them back to shore."

"Now do you see where I get my storytelling abilities?" I said, shaking my head.

"Maybe I could talk you into helping me," kidded Timothy. "It's lambing season, as you can tell. Hey, Uncle Mark," he added, poking Papa in the arm, "didn't you spend a few weeks as a shepherd's assistant when you were Benjamin's age?"

What? My father, a shepherd? Grandfather is a diehard fisherman, and no son of his would ever dream of going near a sheep pen!

"How'd you know that, Timothy?" he said. "Has your father been spilling all my secrets?"

Papa's answer knocked me back to reality. I couldn't believe what I was hearing. "Papa, are you serious? You wanted to be a shepherd?" It was impossible to wrap my brain around Papa's words. In fact, I had always had a mental image of Grandfather wrapping newborn Papa in a linen fishing net instead of swaddling clothes.

"It's sad but true," said Papa, casting a smirk in Timothy's direction. "Your grandfather wanted me to follow in his footsteps and become a fisherman, of course. I wanted to escape the crowds and find a job where I could lie back in the sunshine and be my own boss."

Timothy laughed so hard, I thought we were going to have to resuscitate him.

"And?" I couldn't wait to hear the rest of the story. How could I have lived almost thirteen years and never heard this piece of family history?

"I quickly discovered the truth," said Papa. "After two months as a shepherd's assistant, my boss had to speak to me. For starters, he complained that I kept falling asleep on the job. How'd he expect me to stay awake in such balmy weather? Impossible!"

Timothy was getting a big kick out of Papa's confession. "This is pure entertainment," he joked. "Please continue."

"I didn't like that the sheep were so demanding of my time, either. Trouble struck when I refused to chase after a lamb that had taken off for the third time. I made the mistake of calling it a dumb animal." Papa glanced at Timothy and looked ... well, *sheepish*. "Now, the worse thing a shepherd-in-training can do—"

Timothy finished Papa's sentence. "—is to insult the sheep!"

"So he fired you?" I guessed.

Papa nodded. "He fired me."

I'd grown up hearing Grandfather's version of Papa's life, but it never included anything about sheep. According to him, Papa had "come to his senses" when he was sixteen and joined him the fishing crew. *Thanks for the confession, Papa!* I thought. It might come in handy someday, if I decide to become a shepherd.

Papa stayed until late afternoon. It was obvious that Papa had chosen the right career for him. Every conversation included a reference to fishing. He loves what he does, and he wants me to love fishing, too. When it was time for him to leave, he embraced me and whispered in my ear, "Don't fall asleep on the job, or you might end up a fisherman like your father."

Midnight Stalker

Hey, Journal,

Timothy and I rounded the sheep up and led them into their pen for the night. Some shepherds don't believe in confining their animals, but my cousin does. "Turning them loose at night is too risky," he said. "These hills are teeming with wild animals. There's no sense inviting trouble."

"Why doesn't it have a gate?" I wondered.

"Good question," said Timothy. "Watch this." He laid his shepherd's staff on the ground in the gap where a gate should be. A couple of older sheep investigated like cautious parents locking their front door for the night. Satisfied at last, they rejoined the flock and huddled together for warmth.

"Sometimes I even lie across the gap myself, as a human gate," said Timothy.

Timothy kicked the staff aside and stretched out on his back to demonstrate. An audience of curious sheep ventured over to have a look. Ewes sniffed his hair and hands and inspected the

Bonnie Bruno

rough texture of his warm woolen cape. Babies bucked and leapt playfully all around him until their mothers nudged them back.

"See, Benjamin? Sheep don't care what fills the gap, as long as it's filled."

How great to have a place of total rest—somewhere to feel safe and secure. That's how I feel when I sense God is near. And when I listen—*really* listen—he speaks words of peace to my heart. God watches over my comings and goings like a gentle, caring Shepherd. He is my Gate!

Hey, Journal,

We settled under a wooden lean-to shelter near a toasty fire. The lean-to blocked the chilly north wind and provided a dry spot for our bedrolls. I had a good view of the sheep pen from there, too.

Evening unrolled like a star-studded canopy. Timothy pointed out various stars and reminded me of something Papa had told me when I was little: "God created each star in the heavens, and he calls them by name." Imagine that! I wonder if he has a favorite nickname for me, too.

I wish Uncle Lem could see how happy his son is here. I wish he would find it in his heart to accept Timothy's choice. He ought to be proud that he raised a son whose work brings him such joy. I hope Papa will feel the same about the choice I eventually make. I hope he'll be proud of me whether I become a fisherman, a shepherd, or *whatever*.

Hey, Journal,

We awoke to a hot, muggy morning. "Ughhhh. We're in for a scorcher," said Timothy. He handed me a shepherd's staff formed from a gnarly old grapevine. "I now proclaim you an official shep-herd."

I drew back for a second, not sure what to do with it. "Now what? I mean, do I hold it up like this and wave it at the sheep, or what?"

Timothy laughed at my question. "No, lamebrain. Here, just hold it like a walking stick, a very tall walking stick. Pretend like you know what you're doing. And if you see a wild boar charging us, feel free to whack him with it."

Timothy retrieved his own staff from the entrance to the sheep pen, where it had lain all night. "We're going to lead the flock down the hill to a small freshwater stream. I'll stay in front and you can bring up the rear."

Timothy guided his flock like a seasoned old shepherd. When he stopped and held up his staff, the sheep stopped, too. When he turned to the left, the flock followed. Meanwhile, I kept an eye on them from the opposite side, making sure the younger lambs didn't stray off. A few of them paused occasion-ally to nibble the fresh grass or danced around like playful children.

Once they drank their fill from the cool stream, the sheep grazed for most of the afternoon in a lush green field at the backside of the hill. "As you can see, grass doesn't have a chance to grow very tall around here," said Timothy.

I tried out my best shepherd's call, but the sheep didn't even blink. When Timothy spoke to them, though, they assembled in a group for their venture back up to their hillside pasture. "What can I say, Benjamin?" Timothy said with a shrug. "They look to me as their protector and friend."

Timothy led the sheep back into their pen and laid his staff across the gap. With *baaa-aaaing* as our backdrop, we shared a meal he'd prepared from five secret ingredients. "I call it 'Timothy's Surprise,'" he said. That was enough to worry me! (Every time Mama fixes "Mama's Surprise," it's just another term for leftovers—*lots* of leftovers.)

The sun winked one last time before it slipped over the edge of our world. The sheep sensed the sudden change in temperature and one by one, they settled down in cozy groups to keep warm.

"Nobody has to teach them how to survive; they just instinctively *know*," said Timothy. Truly, God thought of every detail when he created our world.

I wadded up an extra blanket for a pillow. "Wake me if a jackal or wolf shows up," I kidded, "and I'll toss the rest of Timothy's Surprise at 'em!"

"Excellent plan," said Timothy. "Maybe if they get a good taste of my rotten cooking, they'll spread the word and we won't have to worry about midnight stalkers anymore."

"Either that, or they'll beg for your recipe," I told him.

Timothy surveyed the silhouette of surrounding hills. "Seriously, Benjamin, you need to know something. I wasn't kidding about midnight stalkers. We do get a lot of unwanted four-legged visitors up here, usually in the wee hours of the morning."

I was exhausted before he made that announcement, but suddenly I was wide awake. "Okay, I get your message," I said, "but what should I do if I see anything sneaking around here? Lie still, jump up and make a racket, or what?"

"Jackals are sneaky creatures," he said. "You might *feel* their presence long before you actually see them."

"*Their?*" I asked. "As in, more than one jackal at a time?" Shivers ran up my spine at the thought of a whole pack of howling jackals. *They could be out there right now watching us. Waiting. Planning their first sneaky move!*

Timothy positioned his face within inches of mine, close enough for me to see beads of sweat above his lip. "Benjamin, there's something you should know. Jackals travel in packs. I've seen six or eight of them at once."

My heart felt like it was going to jump out of my chest. I sucked in my breath and gasped. "But what did you mean, when you said I'll *feel* their presence?"

"When they lick your face, goofus," he said. "It's hard to ignore a jackal when he's lapping your cheeks." Timothy rolled on the ground and laughed hysterically.

I knew my cousin was a jokester, but how could I be sure he was only kidding this time? I didn't want to come off sounding afraid of my own shadow, so I laughed like I thought it was funny. "Has anyone ever told you that you laugh like a sick hyena?" I asked.

Hey, Journal,

It is impossible to doze with one eye open. I lay there half the night, expecting to be pounced on at any moment. My body eventually gave up the fight and slipped into a deep sleep.

Around midnight, though, something startled me awake. Lying as still as possible, I listened for footsteps or telltale growls. I sniffed the air for signs of anything unusual—the stinky breath of a wild boar or the smell of fear rising up out of the sheep pen. My breaths came faster, and I could hear my heart tapping a panicky rhythm against my cloak.

Bonnie Bruno

A strange noise skittered across the hillside. It sounded crunchy, like someone stepping slowly through dry weeds. I eased up onto one elbow and peered into the darkness. I wasn't imagining; the sheep had heard it, too. In the dim light of a half moon, I could make out the hazy outlines of the flock, pressing in one wiggly mass toward the far corner of the pen. The lambs' bleating grew louder and shriller.

Timothy slept nearby, wrapped up to his ears in his woolen cape. My reaction was going to determine our fate—whether we would live or die by the jaws of our intruder. I knew in my gut that I didn't have time to waste. I must do *something* and do it quickly!

A Friend in Need

Hey, Journal,

I'd like to say that I jumped up and made such a racket, every four-legged predator in the Judean hills took off running at full speed. But in all honesty, I was too petrified to move. My breath slipped out in slow, measured gasps. If that hairy beast heard or smelled or saw me, I was a goner. History. Dinner!

Should I reach over and nudge my cousin? Timothy snored on, oblivious to our intruder. But wait! Wasn't Timothy accustomed to sleeping out in the open every night? Wasn't he used to normal sounds of the hill country? If Timothy hadn't heard anything unusual, then why should I be concerned? Maybe my imagination had run ahead of common sense again.

I took a deep breath of fresh air and tried to calm my thumping heart. Pulling my blanket up around my ears, I rolled over onto my side to face the sheep's pen. A faint, oniony scent hung over our cooking area—a reminder of last night's Timothy's Surprise. If I were a wild animal sneaking about at night, I'd head straight for that cooking pot. We two had been so sleepy after dinner, we decided to leave our dirty dishes until morning. Any self-respecting wild animal would be licking the pot and those bowls, wouldn't he?

I pulled my cloak over both ears and tried to settle back to sleep, but the sheep were growing more restless by the minute. "BAAA-aa! Baaa-AAA!" Their frantic cries rolled down the hillside, echoing back at us from the hill beyond.

Enough was enough! I threw a small rock at my cousin. "Pssst! Timothy, wake up! I think we have company."

Timothy leapt to his feet. "Stay put unless I call for you," he whispered. "Keep the fire stoked, but stick close. No matter what happens, stay by the fire. Promise?"

I croaked a weak agreement. I wasn't sure which was better—sitting there alone by the fire where the beast could see me, or slinking around in the darkness with Timothy.

Didn't he say "no matter what happens"? What did he mean by that? Was he expecting trouble? I needed a plan—any plan! What if a pack of wild jackals turned on him? How could I sit here and not help him? Wouldn't two of us stand a better chance than one?

My hands turned cold and clammy. My head spun from a combination of excitement and dread. I stirred the fire with a long stick, all the while keeping one eye fixed on Timothy. He moved on feet so agile, I knew he'd faced such challenge before. He reminded me of a leopard slinking around the pen.

Flames crackled and sent sparks flying upward, lighting the entire area. On the far side of the pen, a few feet from Timothy, something shadowy and dark drew back and snarled, its teeth gleaming like jewels in the light of the dancing flames. "Timo-

A Friend in Need

thy, look out!" I bellowed.

Sheep piled against each other, pushing forward in an awkward rush to escape. "Timothy! Over there!" I cried again, pointing to a spot near the far corner of the pen.

Timothy took aim with his trusty slingshot—our only weapon on that lonesome hilltop—and let loose with a torrent of stones. The jackal flinched and yelped. It turned tail and tore off into the night.

I fell back like a weary soldier, breathless and sweating.

"Are you alright?" asked Timothy, laughing at my shocked expression. How could he laugh at a time like this?

"I'm okay," I lied, but my shaky hands and knees told the truth. "How did you do that?" I asked.

"Do what?"

Do what? Was he kidding? "I mean, how'd you stay so calm?"

"It's called survival, Benjamin. Shepherding isn't for the weak-kneed. I've been at this for almost three years. I can't let fear paralyze me."

"What should we do now? Won't the jackal come back?" I asked.

"Nope. He must have gotten separated from his pack. Judging from the way he yipped, I think I made a direct hit, don't you?" Timothy kissed his slingshot. "It's the best defense against predators," he said proudly. "It's all I've needed so far, at least."

I trust Timothy, but I trust God more.

"I prayed harder than I've ever prayed," I confessed. "I guess I'm not cut out for this kind of excitement."

"Oh, that's just fear talking," said Timothy. "In time, you'll

Bonnie Bruno

discover how courageous you really are. You kept a cool head tonight, Benjamin. That's a good quality."

I still wasn't convinced that the jackal was gone for good. Timothy curled up on his bedroll. "Get some sleep. Tomorrow's another day," he said.

In case the jackal tried to prove my cousin wrong, I decided to stand watch until dawn. "Go ahead and sleep," I replied. "I'll be your gate for now."

Timothy reached over and squeezed my shoulder. "By the way, thanks for waking me up. You saved my skin. I owe you one, Benjamin."

"They owe me one, too," I said, nodding toward the flock. "That jackal was counting on lamb chops for dinner. And by the way, nice job with the slingshot, Cousin."

Hey, Journal,

Daybreak arrived in a display of crimson streaks that floated heavenward like a morning prayer. Dew-heavy grass wet my toes as I padded across the hill in search of my sandals. Everything about the morning sang of God's faithfulness. Birdsongs spread from tree to tree and hill to hill, awakening the valley below. Flowers woke up and turned their yellow faces toward the sun. A caterpillar inched through the grass on a voyage known only to its Creator. I felt like a survivor, and the whole world looked brighter this morning.

Timothy had already awakened and was busy making his rounds, counting the sheep. I wasn't prepared for the news he was about to deliver. "Our snaggle-toothed visitor must've snatched one of the newborn lambs."

That explained the ewe who had spent the night pacing and crying out for her little one.

"What are we going to do? Is it too late to save the lamb? What if—"

"Benjamin, calm down! You win some and lose some. We'll search for the lamb and if we find it, fine. If we don't, we'll have to let it go and move on."

We counted again to be sure. Sadly, Timothy was right. Its mother bleated noisily for her baby. "She wonders why her lamb isn't nursing this morning," explained Timothy.

I don't know what came over me, but my heart filled with such pity for that poor missing lamb. I volunteered to search for it, without considering the danger. What if I stumbled on that jackal, licking its bloody lips? Or worse yet—what if I ran into a whole pack of jackals, feasting on the lamb like some family celebration?

"Watch for fresh tracks, bits of lamb's wool, or a bloody trail," Timothy suggested. "If you sense danger, come back. Be careful. One little lamb isn't worth risking your life, Benjamin."

Hey, Journal,

Minutes stretched into hours while I searched for the missing lamb. In my heart, I hoped it had only run away in a playful quest to explore the hillside. A runaway would stand a better chance at survival than a lamb that had been chased off by a predator. I hadn't gone far when I realized how unprepared I was for the search.

Why didn't I think to ask Timothy the lamb's name? I called out every sheep name I could imagine, but it was no use. I was a stranger, and the poor lost lamb didn't know my voice. If it happened to be in trouble somewhere close by, it wouldn't trust

Bonnie Bruno

me any more than it would trust a jackal. I hadn't gained its trust.

My imagination painted a dreary picture. What if the lamb had gotten caught in a thorny bush? Would it cry out for help or watch me pass by? The further I hiked, the less I expected to find it. A new lamb would not intentionally wander that far from its source of milk, would it? I could still hear its mother's frantic bleating—a pitiful announcement to the world of her loss.

A thought struck me out of nowhere: Peter is exactly like that lamb! He might be in big trouble, but he doesn't know how to ask for help.

There comes a point when a shepherd has to move on. My time had come. The hardest moment was when I had to admit that the lamb was gone. Lost forever. I changed directions and took a shortcut back up the hill.

A Long-Guarded Secret

Hey, Journal,

"Baaaa-aaa! Baaaa-aaa-aaaaa!" The most beautiful sound in the world jerked me around and sent me hurrying back down the trail.

There I found a frantic, wild-eyed lamb calling out with all its might. "Where have you been?" I said, half laughing and half crying. "I've looked everywhere for you!"

I untangled its feet from a sticker bush, and gathered the quivering little body close. "Calm down, you're going to be fine," I whispered. "I'm taking you home where you belong."

Thank you, God! Thank you! I felt like I'd earned a golden shepherd's staff or a free pass into an exclusive club for shepherds. The lamb pressed its face against me, its soft wool coat tangled with burrs. "Let's go home," I whispered. "Your mama is waiting for you behind the gate."

I delivered the frightened lamb back to its fold. "What a relief!" cried Timothy. "Thanks, Cousin. You've got shepherd's

Bonnie Bruno

blood running through your veins."

Unfortunately, this shepherd had to leave. My time on the hill had ended much too soon.

"I'll miss you," said Timothy. He patted me on the back affectionately. "Remember, you're welcome here anytime."

"Well, I hope my next visit won't be quite as exciting," I joked.

Timothy waved from the crest of the hill, then disappeared from view. I had planned to head home and surprise my family, but I spotted smoke rising from the area of Peter's fort. Was his place on fire?

I found Peter warming his hands over a small fire he'd made from a pile of dried twigs. "You're just in time for breakfast," said Peter. Fresh wild berries added the perfect touch to a bowl of thick porridge .

Reading Peter's moods had become a full-time job. He didn't mention my last visit to his hilltop hideaway. I told him about my two days with my cousin's flock. "I saw the hugest, toothiest jackal ever last night. It must have weighed a hundred pounds, and its paws could have knocked a bear off its feet in one swipe! For a while there, I wasn't sure we'd survive."

"I've had run-ins with jackals a few times myself," said Peter, nodding his head.

"You mean up here—by your fort" I asked.

"Yep. Right where you're sitting, as a matter of fact," said Peter.

Now, I don't claim to be an expert on wild animals, but one thing I do know: Jackals appear at night, after darkness and quiet settle in. "So, you've stayed here overnight? Weren't you scared?"

"Not really. You get used to it after a while."

If I'm famous for anything, it's for having an expressive face. Papa always says that my face is easy to read. "Nobody has to guess what you're thinking," he says.

Peter didn't have to guess, either. He realized he'd opened a door with that last sentence—a door that he would not be able to close. Peter considered his fort a home. He lived there in the cave, no doubt about it.

Lord, where do I go from here? I prayed. God answered with an unmistakable nudge. It was time to ask the question I'd been wanting to ask Peter for months. It was time to lay all the secrets out in the open.

"Peter, can we talk? I need to get something off my chest."

Peter replied in a low voice, as if he knew what was coming next. "I'm a captive audience," he said.

"I learned something awesome when I was working with Timothy yesterday," I said. "Something about his sheep pen."

"Oh, okay, I get it. You're going to give me a list of 100 reasons why you want to become a shepherd, right?" asked Peter. "Number one, it's fun living outdoors. Number two, you don't have to work for a cranky boss. Number three, you can count the stars and nobody will tell you to blow out your lamp and go to bed. Number four ..."

Peter was not making this easy! "Hey Peter, did you know that a true shepherd can lie across the open end of a sheep pen and—"

"—and become a human gate?" said Peter, finishing my sentence. "*Of course* I know that, Benjamin! For your information, my dad *is* a shepherd."

Hey, Journal,

I could hardly believe Peter's news. After all this time, he'd mustered up the courage to tell me the truth. His face reddened, as if he'd accidentally exposed a long-guarded secret.

"You're serious? Your dad's a shepherd? Peter, that's awesome! I would've never thought ... I mean, I thought maybe your parents were—"

"What, dead?" Peter's glare bored a hole through me.

Lord, help me! I prayed. *I don't want to mess this up!*

"It's just that I had no idea your father worked in the hill country," I said. "Every time I ask about your parents, you always look away." I studied Peter's face for a clue to what he was feeling. "Peter, I want to be friends, but sometimes you make it almost impossible."

Peter's reaction surprised me. He didn't get mad. He didn't glance away. He looked me square in the eye and spoke gently, just like a true friend would speak.

"I've wanted to tell you—really I have, Benjamin. You wouldn't believe how many times I've rehearsed this conversation. But every time I got to the point of speaking up, I backed out."

"Am I that much of an ogre?" I laughed. "Hmmm. I think I'm a pretty nice guy, actually. At least my mother thinks so."

Peter cocked his head in the direction of the cave. "Can we talk inside?"

We talked long into the afternoon. Peter shared news so huge, I thought my heart would burst. It both relieved and saddened me.

"My dad is ... I mean, *was* a shepherd," he explained. "After the sickness took over, he couldn't keep up with his work. His brother—my uncle—took over my father's herds and expected me to quit school immediately and work in the fields. I begged for a chance to complete my classes at the synagogue. I need to learn reading and writing. A life without reading and writing would be horrible."

"But your mother—didn't she protest? Didn't she stick up for you?" I can't imagine Mama making me quit school to work. "So, what happened?"

"Synagogue authorities took my parents away. Neighbors turned away—neighbors who had always treated us kindly. As my parents passed down the street, they rushed their kids inside. 'Unclean! Unclean! Coming through!' called the person who led them away."

I wanted to understand. I searched Peter's face for a clue. "But why did your parents have to leave? You said your father was sick."

"Both my parents were—*are*—very sick." His voice trailed off.

"Where are they? Can I meet them?" I asked.

Peter buried his face in his hands. "Benjamin, I wish it were that easy. They live in a colony, away from the rest of us. I'm not allowed near that place."

His next words sent chills up my spine.

"My parents have *leprosy*, Benjamin. It's like something invisible is eating away at their bodies. But the worst part is how leprosy has eaten away at their hearts. They feel dirty and unwanted. They're cut off from the rest of the world."

Peter's news explained everything—the cave, his evasive replies, and the times he rushed off toward the hills like a sheep on the run.

Bonnie Bruno

"But Peter, why didn't you tell me sooner? Why didn't you trust me?" I asked.

Peter's face looked drained of all emotion. "How do you tell someone that your parents are forbidden, off-limits? Nobody would want to talk to me if they knew. They'd treat me as if I were the one with leprosy."

"Not me," I said. Now that the truth was out, my stomach knotted with worry. "Peter, what if your uncle talks to Rabbi and makes you quit school?"

Peter hesitated. He studied my face for a long time, before replying. "Benjamin, don't you get it? My uncle isn't going to change his mind. He doesn't see why a shepherd needs to learn reading and writing. All he knows is that his herds are huge, and he needs more help. Free labor—that's what he's looking for. I'm it."

"But how do you stand living with somebody who doesn't care whether you learn to read or write? How do you stand it, Peter?"

Peter stared me down like he was seeing me for the first time. "Benjamin, listen to me. Look around you. Everything I own is jammed in this cave. I *live* here. Don't you understand? This is my home now."

A Deeper Glimpse

Hey, Journal,

Peter's news caught me off guard, like a sudden bolt of lightning. "So you live here in this cave?" I asked slowly. "All the time?"

Peter nodded. "It's really not so bad, except for when it rains or freezes, which doesn't happen often."

"And your uncle—isn't he searching for you?" I couldn't imagine Uncle Lem just walking away and forgetting about me. He would search until he found me, the way I searched for the lost lamb.

"My uncle doesn't care about me, Benjamin. He doesn't care about my parents, either. Out of sight, out of mind—that's his motto."

Peter's place appeared to have all the basics anyone would need to get by. "But what do you eat? How do you keep your food bin filled?"

"Easy," he said, grinning like he was about to reveal the world's top secret. "I work for it. Rabbi's sister has a garden—"

Bonnie Bruno

"What? So are you saying that Rabbi knows?"

Peter seemed amused by my questions. "Not only does he know, Benjamin, he has given me his full blessing. He 'admires my stamina'—his words exactly."

Peter and I would soon be old enough to make our own way in the world. I guess Peter just had a head start on me.

"And what about my cousin, Timothy?" I said. "You two already knew each other, right?"

Peter rolled his eyes. "Your cousin is the curious type—like you. He tracked me down like a sly fox until I admitted that I lived in this cave." Peter patted a small table near the food bin. "He even helped furnish it," he said. "Your cousin is a good man."

Peter went on to tell me how Timothy often shared food and drink with him. "I've never gone a day without eating well," he said.

"Have you tried his famous 'Timothy's Surprise' yet? That stuff is nasty!"

We shared a good laugh but returned quickly to a sad reality. "I have it easy, compared to my parents' life in the leper colony," said Peter. "At least I can come and go as I please. Nobody calls me names or rushes their children away from me." His voice faded to a whisper. "I wish I could visit them. As far as everyone else is concerned, they're outcasts, filthy diseased throwaways. I miss them so much, Benjamin!"

Peter's story didn't end there. "I have two sisters and a younger brother, too. Last I heard, they were moving to Jerusalem with my mother's cousin. When I'm able to make a living for myself, I'm going to visit them."

I've never felt so helpless. Nothing I could say would make

a difference. I couldn't change anything about his parents' illness. I couldn't reunite his family. But I could offer him a place to run when he felt lonely or uncertain. Mama had already extended an open invitation. "Peter, you're welcome at my house anytime. My parents have been badgering me to invite you. Will you come sometime?"

He nodded his acceptance. "Sometime soon, maybe I will."

I needed to go. The walk home would give me time to sort out all I'd learned about my friend. *Friend.* The word had a nice new ring to it. In a few short minutes, our relationship had changed from classmates to heart-to-heart friends. Thank you, Lord, for giving me a deeper glimpse into Peter's life.

Hey, Journal,

Peter and I met after school. "My mom has something for you. Can you stop by my house on your way ... uh, on your way ... ."

"Home?" said Peter, jumping in to rescue me. "It's okay, Benjamin. I have a home. It just looks different than most houses, that's all."

I could have kicked myself. Why do I bumble around like that? Peter was right; his home on the hill is as much a home to him as my modest walled house is to me.

"Well, let me think," said Peter, putting on a fake dignified voice. "I don't seem to have anything on my social calendar for today. Sure, I could stop by."

Peter's twisted sense of humor lightened our steps. "You're weirder than weird," I said.

Peter pretended to flinch from my comment. "Takes one to know one."

We passed by the marketplace, where out-of-town merchants

were hawking their wares. "Fresh olive oil! Get your fresh olive oil, straight from the press!" announced a wrinkled old merchant. His head cloth had slipped to one side, giving him a cockeyed appearance.

"Dates and figs! Name your price!" shouted the merchant in the next booth.

"Name your price, and he'll up it," whispered Peter. "It's all part of the game. I guess that's why they're merchants and not fishermen. They love to bargain."

"Well, today you're going to get the best bargain of the week," I said. "Mama is a great cook."

Mama greeted Peter warmly with a hug. "I've been wanting to meet you," she said. "Benjamin has been bragging about his friend, the genius." She cut us each a thick slice of warm onion bread. "Sit, sit!" she said, pulling out a stool at the table for Peter.

Mama knows all about Peter's family situation. She cried when I first explained it to her. I made her promise that she'd treat him just like she treated me. "No tears, please! Peter wants to be treated the same as everyone else." So she turned her tears into smiles, instead. I'm so proud of her.

Lydia took to Peter like an ant to a tree stump. "Do you know any good stories" she asked. "Benjy tells me stories all the time."

"Benjy?" he said with a grin. "Awww, how cute."

Thanks a lot, Lydia!

Peter told Lydia a drawn-out tale of marauding wolves and runaway sheep. "The father and son used their staffs to pull their sheep back to safety."

"And they lived happy every day after that?" asked Lydia.

"Every day," said Peter.

Peter and his dad had spent time in the fields together tending their flock. One day together, the next day apart. Life can change in an instant. Maybe that's why Rabbi teaches us to rejoice at each sunrise and to count our blessings even when we feel like complaining.

Mama lugged a basket over to the table and set it next to Peter.

"Here, take some food off my hands," she said. "Our ancient pear tree out back—a wild, stubborn tree that won't give up—is dropping more fruit than we'll ever use. I tossed a few apricots and dates in there, too. Oh, and olive oil. A kitchen isn't complete without olive oil."

Peter seemed overwhelmed by the outpouring of affection. "Wow! I hardly know what to say."

"Say you'll come to dinner tomorrow," said Mama. "It would give us all a chance to get better acquainted. Benjamin's papa will be home from the sea, and I'm sure he'd love to meet you, Peter."

Peter accepted the invitation. (Is this the same kid who evaded every single question just a couple of weeks ago?) "I'd love to," he said, "but only if Lydia will tell *me* a story."

Lydia blushed. "I know one about *Benjy!*" she squealed. "It's very, very, VERY funny. And it really happened, too!"

Peter smirked. "I can hardly wait," he said, rubbing his hands together.

Hey, Journal,

I spent the evening studying my lesson for tomorrow. If these walls could talk, they'd beg me to go to bed. I must have recited my lesson twenty times or more. If Rabbi calls on me, my perfect recitation is going to curl his silver beard.

Mama acted quiet and edgy after Peter left today. She hates that he lives way up on that desolate hill by himself. "Timothy is just a hill away," I assured her. "In fact, they already know each other."

Papa will be home from the sea tomorrow. I can hardly wait to hear his fish stories. He's been hinting about taking me out on the water soon. "Once you haul in your first catch, you'll be hooked," he says.

The only thing I'm hooked on is shepherding. Will Papa ever understand?

Where's Peter?

Hey, Journal,

I awoke early to recite my lesson one more time. "I'm proud of you, Benjamin," said Mama. "You've been studying hard, and it shows."

"The walls are my witness," I joked. "They're about to crumble from all this rehearsing."

Mama tucked a dried flower in my lunchbox. "It's a special blessing over your day," she said. Papa never misses an opportunity to bless his family, but with him gone so much, Mama picks up the slack. If one of her children needs encouraging, she steps in and blesses us.

Today's Scripture recitation reminds me of Peter's life. "The person who rests in the shadow of the Most High God will be kept safe by the Mighty One," reads Psalm 91. "I will say about the Lord, 'He is my place of safety. He is like a fort to me. He is my God. I trust in him.'"

Peter's real fort—his "place of safety"—is not that cave on

the hill. God will remain long after Peter leaves that temporary shelter. I hope he learns to trust in God the way I do. I repeated the psalm on my way to school and felt its truth fill me up like a warm meal.

Usually, I try to avoid Rabbi's gaze by looking away, but that always seems to backfire. This morning, though, I was so prepared I couldn't wait for him to call on me. He'll plant his big feet right in front of my seat and ask me to recite the day's Scripture passage. But there I sat, feeling all intelligent and smug, and what did he do? He passed me by! I felt like sticking my foot out to stop him.

I refused to give up. I sighed as loud as possible and waved my hand around. Short of groveling on the floor at his feet, I could do nothing more to get his attention—until a brilliant idea popped into my head. Rabbi was making his way around the classroom again, taking his sweet time. Right before he got to me, I grabbed my stomach and leaned forward. "I think I'm going to be sick!" I bellowed.

You should've seen him move. Grabbing my elbow, he ushered me outside to a bare, dusty area behind the synagogue. I gulped air like a fish out of water.

"Feeling better, Benjamin?" Rabbi finally asked. His eyes squinted concern, but I could feel him secretly probing my brain for clues. He pressed his palm over my forehead. "Well, thanks be to God, you're not feverish."

If I didn't hurry, I'd miss my golden opportunity, so I cleared my throat and spoke in a weak voice. "Rabbi, Sir? I studied my lesson last night. Want to hear it?" I didn't wait for him to answer, but dove right in: 'The person who rests in the shadow of the Most High God ... '

Rabbi's bushy eyebrows twitched. He closed his eyes and (I am not kidding!) *swayed*, as if he was going to faint. His beard didn't curl as I'd hoped, but my perfect recitation did drag a compliment out of him. "Wonderful!" he cried, clapping his hands. "Benjamin, look what happens when you set your mind to studying!"

We'd almost reached the classroom when he leaned down and whispered, "Feeling a lot better now?" He winked at me and added, "By the way, have I ever told you that you remind me of myself when I was your age?"

Hey, Journal,

I lingered around the tree where Peter and I usually meet after school, but he didn't show up. I asked a classmate if he'd seen him. "Yes, he left about midway through class, when you were sick. He said he had to hurry—something about a special appointment he needed to keep."

That's odd; Peter didn't mention anything to me about an appointment. I shrugged it off and decided to ask him about it when he came to my house for dinner.

Mama fixed a delicious meal of cardamom chicken livers and potato pastries. How I love those baked circles of buttery dough, filled with mashed potatoes and onions. She topped the meal off with a family favorite that Peter was going to love. Mama makes this noodly pudding and fills it with sour cream, chopped apples, dates, raisins, and walnuts. Sometimes she tosses in apricots or figs, too. I wonder how long it's been since Peter's lips touched a dessert like that?

Papa and my brothers arrived home mid-afternoon, dirty and tired. Before he ever spoke, I could tell that his three days on the sea must have been a wild success. Papa's grin seemed to wrap halfway around his head. "We caught too many fish to count," he said, "but I'd guess they numbered in the hundreds."

"So, did my net hold out?" I asked. According to Micah and Abe, I've gained quite a reputation as a supreme net-mender. Not bad for a first-timer, if I say so myself!

A delicious aroma permeated the house. "Martha, if you cook any more dishes, the neighbors are going to think we're celebrating the birth of a baby!" Papa chuckled. He planted a kiss on Mama's neck.

"Not a chance!" she said. "I have two healthy sons who are old enough to marry and give us grandchildren, though. Micah and Abe, are you listening?" teased Mama.

Papa peeked out at the darkening sky. Sunset was just minutes away, and Peter still had not arrived. Peter doesn't live far. What could possibly be taking him so long?

"Are you sure he remembers the way to our house?" asked Papa.

Each day at sundown, Papa follows a tradition of gathering our family around the table. He offers a prayer, thanking God for watching over us and asking him to bless our home. "It is time to begin," said Papa. Papa lit the oil lamp and set it on its lamp stand. Light danced across the table as he lifted his voice in prayer. At the close of his prayer, he declared that God would forever remain our faithful provider. Softly he added, "And we trust you are providing for our friend Peter this evening, too."

Mama's potato pastry melted in my mouth. My father and two hungry brothers made sure they didn't leave any leftovers.

Where's Peter?

I lost my appetite and passed on the pudding. The empty chair beside me was a constant reminder of Peter's rude absence. Mama was worried that something terrible had happened, but by the time I went to bed, I felt more angry than worried. How dare he accept an invitation and not show up!

Hey, Journal,

A loud knock sent Papa hurrying to the door early this morning. "Who in the world would bother me at this hour?" he grumbled.

I heard Papa speak in a low voice. "Give me a minute to dress. I'll be right out."

Probably a neighbor in need of help. Papa rarely has time to himself. Let anyone in our neighborhood spot him home from his work on the seashore, and they ask to borrow him for a repair here or a bit of advice there. Papa is a popular fixture in town, a rare friend who cannot find it in his heart to say no.

"People need a hand now and then. God knows how many kind hearts have helped me along the way," I heard him tell Mama. Papa wears that statement like a motto.

His words pricked my conscience this morning, since I wasn't feeling very kindly toward Peter. He had let us all down, and I'm going to give him a gigantic piece of my mind the next time I see him.

Peter didn't show up for school. It was impossible to concentrate, and Rabbi's words sailed right over my head and out the door. The minute he dismissed class, I charged out the door and ran all the way to the hill.

Fishing for Friendship

Hey, Journal,

My imagination scurried ahead of me like a panicky field mouse. Had a bloodthirsty jackal or bear tried to reclaim its cave home? Had Peter had an accident and fallen into a deep gully?

I found Peter relaxing in the shade of an old fig tree, whittling away on a stick. "Hey, Benjamin!" he said, jumping to his feet. "What brings you up here to the top of the world?"

I glared at him. Is he really that clueless? "Well, it seems like I'm the one who ought to be asking questions! For starters, since when do you accept an invitation to dinner and not show up?"

Peter's cheeks turned as red as his pile of pomegranates. "I just couldn't handle it, that's all." He pointed to the fruit. "Help yourself to one."

I ignored his hospitality. "What do you mean, you couldn't 'handle it'? Handle what—my family's kindness? A homemade meal? A warm home instead of a leaky old cave?"

Peter looked like I'd smacked him, but it was too late to take back my outburst.

"Peter, I just don't understand you. One moment you share your problems with me like a real friend. Then you turn around and spit in my face."

I half expected him to throw a major fit, but his answer surprised me. "You're right, as usual. I don't have an excuse, Benjamin. I wanted to come to your house—really I did—but I couldn't. Maybe we should just be friends at school and leave it at that."

The more Peter talked, the madder I got. God stepped in and whispered words of peace to calm me down: *Take a deep breath, Benjamin. Peter needs compassion, not an accusing finger.*

I heard myself say, "Are you kidding? A part-time friendship would be a joke. We're going to be friends all the time or not at all. Got that?"

Peter looked puzzled. "Okay, whatever you say."

I wanted him to understand that I was a loyal friend, and nothing—not even a stupid mistake—could change that. Tomorrow was a perfect opportunity to prove it, too. "Hey Peter, there's no school tomorrow. I was thinking of going fishing. Want to come along?"

"Nah. I'd probably get seasick and throw up all over the place. Me and boats don't get along."

"That's impossible," I said, shaking my head. "You can't get seasick unless you're out on the sea. We're going to fish where we won't need a boat. I'm taking you to my top-secret pond."

Peter responded the way I hoped he would. "Sounds like fun. When are you leaving?"

"First thing tomorrow. Bring yourself and a fishing pole. I'll bring lunch. Meet me at the turnoff."

Hey, Journal,

It felt good to talk things out with Peter yesterday. We learned how to be honest with each other without being hurtful. He even told me that I'm full of hot air, and that I exaggerate when I tell all those "tall tales" at school. His words stung a bit, but I'd rather hear them from a friend like Peter than from one of the kids at school who hardly knows me.

"Well, if my so-called tall tales are so boring, why does everyone else laugh at them? Hmmm?"

Peter couldn't look me in the eye. "Benjamin, I hate to tell you this, but they're laughing at *you*, not at your stories."

Now, *that* hurt! I'm not sure I believe him, either.

Today's too nice to worry about it, though. God could not have planned a more perfect day for our outing. "Getting there is half the fun," I told Peter. We met other early-risers along the way, too: rabbits, chattering tree squirrels, and a turtledove leading her seven little ones on a morning walk through the damp grass. A pair of ospreys circled high above the pond. "They're fishing for breakfast," I said.

"Well, let's hope they saved some fish for us," said Peter.

Hey, Journal,

The best thing about fishing is how it empties a person's head. Hard feelings faded while we waited for a fish to tug at our lines. Grudges disappeared when a fish leapt out of the water to grab a well-aimed hook. Fishing with Peter was like rubbing balm on a blistered burn. I hoped he felt the same.

Bonnie Bruno

We stayed at the pond until the fish stopped biting. Most of the time, the fish outsmarted us and escaped our hook. We only caught two fish, but agreed that it was worth the trip.

"Want to fry them for lunch?" suggested Peter.

"Sounds good!" I said. "My mother packed some small bread rolls for us, too. Oh, and she said to be sure to tell you that you're welcome at our house anytime." I was tempted to add, " ... even though you didn't show up for dinner the other night," but I didn't.

We hauled our lunch back to Peter's place on the hill. When we started up the winding path to the top, he pointed to a trickle of smoke drifting skyward above the hill. "My breakfast fire is still going strong," he said.

We cleaned our fish, then laid them on a rack over the fire. The red-hot embers sputtered and glowed, and a determined breeze blew the delicious aroma northward.

While our fish cooked, I walked to the edge of the hilltop and peered out over the land below. "Hey, check this out!" I called to Peter. "It looks like a wedding celebration."

The usually quiet hill country was bustling with activity, families snaked up the side of the hillside opposite ours. Off in the distance, I spotted the Sea of Galilee stretched out like a gigantic puddle. Few afternoons were as beautiful as this one. I tried to freeze the view in my head to take out on rainy, gray days.

I could get used to living up here if I had to, I thought. But I sure couldn't adjust to life without my family. I wanted to ask Peter what his family was like, but thought he might think I was too snoopy. Some people ask questions just so they can gossip, but not me. So I asked.

"Oh, you'd like my parents, Benjamin. They're smart and funny, too. My dad tells stupid jokes—you know, the kind that make everyone groan? And Mom always loved—*loves*—fresh flowers. I remember one winter when she was so desperate to fill her vase, she gathered a bouquet of greenery. I reminded her that they were weeds, and she agreed. 'We'll just pretend they're flowers,' she said."

"Can you visit them sometime?" I asked.

"The leper colony is closed to outsiders, because leprosy is so contagious." A tear escaped and rolled down his cheek. "I worry that they might think I've forgotten them. I want to see them, but can't. That's just the way it has to be, I guess."

"I'm sorry, Peter," I said. "It must feel like a nightmare. I'm really, really sorry."

I've heard the word "leprosy," but I know little about it. People speak in hushed tones, as if the word itself could make them sick. Well, if my parents had leprosy, I would shout it from the rooftops! One way or another, I would make people understand.

"When they took my parents away, my mother's hands, arms, and face were covered with infected sores," said Peter. "They were like thickened patches of skin that eventually went numb. Four of her fingers were so diseased, she couldn't use them anymore." He shook his head at the memory. "It was horrible, Benjamin! Leprosy deformed my father's feet, too, and twisted the features of his face. By the time he entered the colony, I hardly recognized him."

If it helped Peter to talk, I was all ears. It was the only help I could offer. "You said your father was a shepherd, right?" I asked.

Bonnie Bruno

"The best!" said Peter. "He had one of the biggest flocks around and loved his animals almost as much as he loved people. Everything I know about shepherding I learned from him."

"No wonder you and Timothy are friends," I told him. I felt a stab of guilt for the way I'd acted the day we helped Timothy search for his three missing lambs.

"My dad used to say that strangers are just friends-in-waiting."

Friends-in-waiting. I like the sound of that. It reminds me of something my own dad might say. "Your dad and mine would have been good friends, I'll bet," I told Peter. "They sound a lot alike."

"Yeah, except your dad loves the sea as much as my dad loved—*loves*—the hill country. Maybe that's why I don't mind living here on the hill. It makes me feel closer to him."

With My Own Eyes

Hey, Journal,

I tried to find words to say how sorry I was, but my mind drew a blank. Sympathetic words won't help reunite his family. They won't lift the curse of that dreaded disease. For the rest of their days, Peter's parents will be known as "unclean," and their children will wear the label of a leper's child. Why did leprosy touch Peter's family and not mine? Why do awful things happen to one person, but not to another? There seems to be no answer.

Words of sympathy seemed useless, so I sat beside Peter in silence. Silence has a way of healing deep wounds.

Peter was the first to speak. "What are we sitting here for? Come on, let's see what's going on. If we hurry, we might get a front-row seat!"

"A seat to *what?*" I asked. "For all we know, those people are holding a secret meeting to overthrow the Roman governor."

Peter couldn't resist. He groaned. "Uh-oh, do I hear a tall

Bonnie Bruno

tale coming on? I thought you'd given up tall-tale telling."

"It might be tall, but it's not a tale. Seriously, Peter, we have no idea why all those people are gathered over there. When's the last time a crowd that size wandered out into sheep country? If you ask me, something very peculiar is going on."

We blazed our own trail up the next hill and settled on a flat, grassy spot with a magnificent view. Parents reminded young children to stay away from the edge. Older couples chatted about local politics. Peter asked a woman sitting near us, "What's the occasion?"

"Haven't you heard?" she replied. "Someone saw Jesus and his band of friends get out of a boat and head this way. I came to get a good look at our long-awaited Messiah!"

"That's right!" a young father spoke up. "Jesus is going to show these Roman leaders a thing or two. It's about time someone stood up to this rotten government!"

Peter spoke up. "All you people can think about is what you want Jesus to do for you. Take, take, take! What a sorry lot!"

The man dismissed Peter's comment with a wave of his hand. "Everywhere Jesus goes, people are healed. Lives are changed. Sit tight, you'll see it for yourself."

"But Peter, let me ask you something," I said. "If Jesus stood right here beside you, wouldn't you reach out for healing like the lame man did that day?"

He wouldn't hear of it. "Why do I need healing, Benjamin? Look at me—I'm already a survivor. Nobody had to help me, either. I just did what I had to do on my own." My heart sank. Does Peter really think he manages on his own? How quickly he's forgotten the people God has placed across his path— Rabbi, Timothy, and Rabbi's sister, who provided fresh fruits and vegetables.

I hoped we would get a closer look at Jesus this time. I couldn't help but wonder, though: Is Jesus the long-awaited Messiah, or is he just an ordinary man? Can we really know for sure?

Hey, Journal,

When I'm old and wrinkled and too frail to climb these Judean hills, I'll close my eyes and picture the moment Jesus stepped into view. I'll remember him holding his arms out wide, as if to embrace every person there. I'll still feel the wind in my face and the warmth of his smile.

Peter and I had waited so long to see him, we about gave up. He tries to avoid tight crowds, and the clamor of noisy kids and restless adults was wearing on his nerves. "If Jesus doesn't show up in five minutes, I'm leaving," whispered Peter. "It's not like I have nothing better to do with my day, you know."

He'd barely finished his sentence when thirteen men made their way through the gathering. Twelve of them sprawled on a patch of grass like weary travelers. One stood before us— Jesus! His eyes turned toward the crowd—gentle eyes that spread peace and love in one sweeping glance. The more enthusiastic members of the audience broke into a spontaneous chant: "Jesus! Jesus! Jesus!" Peter and I sat there, awed by his presence.

"Is that really him, Papa?" asked a little boy in front of us. His father hoisted him to his shoulders for a better view. "Yes, son, that's Jesus—our Messiah." Tears of joy rolled down the man's face and he ignored them. Who *was* this Jesus, who could make a grown man cry?

A holy hush settled over the hillside. Jesus held out his arms to greet the multitude in a silent embrace One by one, families rose up and carried their sick loved ones to lay at Jesus' feet. And one by one, Jesus healed them by his touch.

I witnessed miracle after miracle. A little girl Lydia's age had arrived there without a voice, but left singing! An elderly woman skipped back and forth like a child after Jesus restored her legs. She had been carried up the hill on a stretcher, but left on her own two feet!

A young man gazed for the first time into the faces of his family, who had watched Jesus restore his sight. "I can see! I can see! Thank you, Jesus! I can see!" he cried. His eyes searched his world for new delights—wispy clouds floating across the sky, grass bending beneath the wind, and the smile on his mother's face.

The day stretched into early evening. Children complained that they were hungry. Some had inched forward to see Jesus up close before they had to go home for dinner. But Jesus had other plans. He asked us all to sit down. Then he turned to his disciples and told them to gather enough food to feed all of us.

Peter rolled his eyes. "Oh, boy. This I gotta see," he said with a smirk.

"Psssst, Peter!" I whispered. "Hand me our basket." I lifted the cloth and sure enough—we had a couple of small loaves leftover from our lunch. One of Jesus' helpers accepted the bread and added it to the food they'd already gathered. He tallied up the amount of food: seven loaves and a few small fish.

Jesus blessed and broke the fishes and loaves. He asked his helpers to pass the food around in baskets. Word spread quickly, and people responded by either waiting expectantly or shaking their heads in disbelief.

One onlooker scolded those who murmured. "You saw him heal the blind and lame, so why do you disbelieve him now? Is anything too hard for him?"

Baskets of food made the rounds from family to family. *What a story this will be!* I thought. I could hardly wait to rush home to tell my family what I'd seen with my own eyes. I would have never believed a story like this if I'd heard it secondhand.

The baskets never emptied—not once! Those seven loaves and a few puny fish fed the entire crowd. In fact, after everyone had eaten their fill, Jesus called for his disciples to collect the baskets. Seven of the baskets contained leftovers!

I nudged Peter and in a fake news-reporter voice asked, "Excuse me, Sir. How would you describe today's feeding of the multitude?"

Peter looked like someone who had been snatched from a deep pit. "I am stunned. Totally-and-forever amazed by what I've witnessed." Peter couldn't take his eyes off Jesus. He studied his movements and hung onto every word as if it were a life raft.

We stayed long after the crowd broke up, standing there at the edge of the hill to watch Jesus and his friends return to the seashore. There they climbed into a boat and sailed across the Sea of Galilee.

"Oh look, he's leaving," Peter said sadly. Peter struggled to speak. "I feel different, Benjamin, sort of like I've witnessed a rescue or something. Only the one who was rescued was *me!*"

Peter watched until the boat sailed out of sight across the water. "I wish Jesus could have stayed longer."

"He'll be back," I said. "I'm sure of it."

Bonnie Bruno

A Place to Begin

Hey, Journal,

Darkness closed in fast, and I was afraid my parents would be worried if I didn't show up soon. I spotted the soft light of home and braced myself for a good scolding, but Mama hugged me instead. "I'm sorry I'm late," I said, "but you should have seen what I saw today!"

She pressed her hand to my mouth. "I was there, too, Benjamin. In fact, all of us—Papa, Grandfather, Micah, Abe, and Lydia—were there."

"So was the crew," said Micah. He looked grubby in his fishing clothes, but hadn't had time to change. "When we saw Jesus heading towards the hill, we followed the crowd to the hillside."

Emotions ran high as each of us shared the highlight of our day. "At first I wasn't sure what to expect from Jesus," I admitted, "but then I saw a blind man healed—with my very own eyes! I saw a lame grandmother leap for joy. It was real. I know it was real!"

"Jesus touched one of the crew members and healed his broken wrist," said Micah, snapping his fingers. "Just like *that!* It happened in an instant, all because he asked and believed."

"I think Peter was healed, too," I said quietly.

Abe rolled his eyes and let out a long sigh. "Whoa boy, here we go. We might as well settle in for one of Benjamin's long-winded stories."

"Afraid not, Abe," I said. "This one's for real. Peter climbed that hill today with his head full of doubt. He left with something he's never felt before—hope. I'm happy for him."

I shared the story of Peter's family and how he ended up living alone on the hill.

"Oh, dear God," said Mama, "I had no idea." Her motherly instinct took over, and she began listing ways we could rescue Peter.

"Mama, he's fine. Rabbi and others are helping him. He has dreams of becoming a shepherd like his father." My own words made me flinch. "I mean, like his father used to be."

Papa and Grandfather exchanged a long glance, as if they had a secret plot. "Listen, Benjamin," Papa began, "that reminds me—"

I couldn't handle another speech about fishing, at least not today. I didn't want to become a fisherman. I didn't want to join the burly crew on the boat. As much as I loved my father and grandfather, I had to choose work that fit me best.

"Papa, please, can we talk about this another time?"

Grandfather laughed out loud. "Oh, so now we're a story-teller and a mind reader, are we? Fascinating!"

I don't like feeling cornered, especially in front of everyone like that.

"Well, no offense," I said, "but I'll be turning thirteen next week. And in case you haven't noticed, I haven't told any so-called 'tall tales' lately."

"I know!" shouted Lydia. "You never tell me good stories anymore, Benjy!"

Papa slung his arm over my shoulder. "Ugh!" I cried. "You smell like fish and sweat."

"And you smell like sheep," said Papa, holding his nose.

Grandfather's eyes sparkled with a secret. "Follow me, Benjamin. It's high time we had a little talk. Just for the fun of it, we're going to blindfold you."

I've learned that you never question a family member who's about to surprise you. A ruined surprise makes everybody mad.

I followed my father and his father outside to a pen that hadn't been used in years. Grandfather led me through the gate, then removed my blindfold. "They're all yours," he said with a shout. Lit only by a well-aimed moonbeam, the pen housed not one ... not two ... but *eight* chubby lambs. They rose one by one from their warm heap to nuzzle my hand hungrily.

I opened my mouth to speak, but nothing would come out. A gift of sheep—from two lifelong fishermen? Impossible! Was I dreaming? Was it a joke?

"He's speechless!" howled Grandfather. "Our official family storyteller is speechless!"

Papa drew me close in a whiskery hug. "Follow your heart, son," he said. "It wouldn't feel right to chase after somebody else's dream. I'm a fisherman, and you're not; but you're twice the shepherd I ever dreamed of becoming."

I recalled Papa's confession—how he had longed to tend

Bonnie Bruno

sheep instead of pulling nets full of fish out of the sea. But the Lord had different plans for his life. "God eventually showed me a different path, that's all," he said. "He has one for you, too."

Grandfather agreed. "Your path leads to the hill this side of Timothy's. That plot of land is yours if you're interested," he said.

Micah and Abe stepped out of the shadows. "We'll even help you build a shelter and a sheep pen," said Micah. "Just don't ask us to chase down strays."

Abe wagged his finger at me. "And you're on your own when it comes to tracking jackals or wrestling bears!"

Hey, Journal,

This morning at school, Rabbi paced the perimeter of our classroom, deciding who to call on next. His knuckles, long callused from years of head-thumping, skipped my head and landed on the boy seated next to me. "Are you in there, young man?" he asked. It seems like only yesterday that Rabbi was asking me the same question.

My thirteenth birthday whizzed by in a blur, and my studies with Rabbi will soon be over. My eight lambs have grown into sheep that will eventually multiply into a bigger flock. I'm going to be a shepherd—a *shepherd!* Papa and Grandfather's gift changed my life, and I accepted it with their full blessing. I'm now free to follow my own dream, instead of the dream they used to have for my life.

As for Peter, he'll soon be completing his studies, too. Even though he discovered a new sense of peace after meeting Jesus, his problems didn't disappear overnight. He still lives on the hill, isolated from his family and his world. He hopes for a better life, but still isn't sure which way to turn.

Tonight Peter came over for dinner. "What are your plans?" Papa asked him. My father was not the prying sort, and I detected a genuine concern for my friend. Peter shifted uncomfortably. "I'm not sure," he admitted. "I haven't thought about it much. Maybe I'll see if Timothy needs help with his flock."

Papa cleared his throat. "Or maybe you'd like to try your hand at fishing. You're welcome to join our crew for awhile, Peter. Try it; you might like it. Most people either love or hate it the first time out. Right, Benjamin?"

A few months ago, Papa's remark would have embarrassed me, but not today. I don't feel the urge to brag or tell exaggerated stories to feel important anymore. If I had been the only person on the hillside that day, I think Jesus still would have followed the trail to the top for a private meeting with me!

Sometimes when I lie in bed at night, I imagine what life would be like if Jesus had not come. The lame grandmother would not be walking today. The blind man would not be admiring sunsets or watching the sun rise on all his tomorrows. The deaf little girl wouldn't be able to hear raindrops tapping her roof or the laughter of friends. If Jesus had not come, Peter would still feel hopelessly stuck. Yes, he's still the son of lepers. He still aches for his family. But hope has unlatched the gate to his future.

Jesus' visit touched my life, too. He made me feel like life has purpose—that I am not here by mistake. When he gazed out over the crowd that day, I know he saw more than just a mass of people; his gaze reached each person, young and old, rich and poor. He saw our needs and he read our hearts. And what's more, Jesus knew we were coming before any of us ever trudged up that hill. He was *expecting* us!

Bonnie Bruno

When he touched the eyes of the blind man, Jesus didn't see a man who had stumbled around in darkness for decades. He saw him healed and whole. When he saw me sitting there, he didn't see a kid who talks too much and listens too little. He saw my good qualities and the plan he has for my life. He knew the dreams buried deep in my heart.

I can hardly wait for my very first night there on my own hillside. I'll tuck my eight sheep inside their pen and lie in the soft grass as a human gate. They'll memorize my voice as I call them by name. And for the rest of their days, I'll lead them by day and watch over them by night like the gentle shepherd I've always longed to become.

Life Issue: **I want to be able to be rest in God.**

Spiritual Building Block: **Hope**

Do the following activities to help increase your level of hope.

Think About it:

Problems have a way of coloring our moods. On a week when everything is going smoothly, the sky seems bluer, people seem friendlier, and the future seems brighter. Then along comes a problem to mess everything up. Sound familiar?

Everyone experiences setbacks sometimes; they're a part of life. If we could schedule our problems at a more convenient time, do you think it would make them easier to accept? Probably not. A problem can make us feel isolated, stuck in a corner with no way out. We might even feel like nobody understands or cares about our situation. And perhaps the toughest part of all is not knowing how long we'll be stuck in that dark, lonely place.

What a blessing to realize that God doesn't view our setbacks the way we do! In fact, sometimes he *allows* a problem into our life to teach us something valuable. He understands that the most lasting lessons—the ones that teach us about his faithfulness—are learned through trials. Tough times are temporary. They provide an opportunity for us to draw closer to God, depending on how we react to them. Romans 12:12 (NIrV) instructs us, "When you hope, be joyful; When you suffer; be patient. When you pray, be faithful."

Are you a whiner? Do you automatically shake your fist at God and let loose with a list of reasons why you don't deserve to suffer so? Do you remind him of all you've done for him and all the times you've shared his love with people in need?

Are you a pouter? When trouble lands on your doorstep, do you automatically assume that God must have surely made a mistake? Do you remind him of all the people you know who are more deserving of such a disappointing detour? Like a stubborn child, do you mentally slam doors and stomp your feet, hoping he'll notice how mad you are, and then change his mind?

God's love for us never changes. He doesn't get a kick out of watching us struggle, but he does love when we turn to him. He doesn't plop us down in the middle of a crisis only to desert us. He walks through every trial alongside us, guiding our steps and assuring us we'll make it through.

Certain problems may appear as a result of our own poor choices. Others are allowed as a means of testing our devotion and trust. We might never learn the reason behind a trial, but that's okay, too. Nothing drives us to our knees in prayer or sends us running for God's Word as much as crisis. When we seek the Lord, problems shrink as hope increases, and hope appears as we turn over bigger chunks of our life to his control.

Are you facing an unexpected crisis this week? Has it changed your view of God? How? Are you wasting time worrying, or using the time to pull in close and listen—*really listen*—to what he wants to teach you? Admit your helplessness and watch God plant a sense of renewed hope in your heart today.

Bonnie Bruno

Talk About it:

Think of a time when the bottom seemed to drop out of your carefully planned week. Can you remember your first reaction? If you knew then what you know now, would you have handled the problem differently?

Is your level of hope like a penlight on a key chain, or like a string of lights on an airport runway? Does your faith in God's ability to handle your future affect your everyday outlook? How?

Don't wait until a crisis hits to get better acquainted with the Lord. Set aside a block of uninterrupted time to see what the Bible has to say about hope. Hope is not the same as wishing; it's the assurance that our eternal God will carry out his promises—no matter what comes our way.

Try it:

Draw a picture of a hat rack on a large sheet of poster board. If hope were a hat rack, what would your family hang on it? Discuss the difference between things that are temporal (temporary) and those that are eternal. Is your hat rack out of balance?

Consider ways you can spread hope to those around you. Offering hope doesn't cost money. It costs time and a willingness to reach out to people who might not necessarily return your cheerful outlook. It means praying before you go and asking God to translate your intentions into the heart of the one who receives a blessing. Imagine yourself cornered, feeling as though nobody cares. What kind of outreach would make you feel most hopeful? An encouraging letter? An anonymous bag of groceries left on a porch? An offer to babysit or weed a garden?

And if you are the one in need of hope today, try reaching out to someone else and watch what happens. It's impossible to worry while God is using you to bless someone else!

Deborah's Secret Journal

If you thought *Ben's Secret Journal* was great, wait until you read *Deborah's Secret Journal*. But you don't have to wait at all—here's a sneak peak at this exciting adventure also releasing September 2004.

• SAMPLE CHAPTER •

If This Vase Could Speak

Dear Journal,

You'd think I'd be dancing and singing, but I feel strangely lost without Salome tugging at my sleeve. I woke up every few minutes last night, partly because I miss my sister, but mostly because I was cold. I thought of her in her own little bed at Aunt Tara's. Was she homesick? Did she peek up at the moon tonight? When they tucked her in bed, did she teach them our special "Under the Moon" song?

Look at me—I'm pathetic! One day I complain because I'm tired of Salome trailing me around, and now I'm lying awake in the middle of the night, worried that she might be homesick. If she has one of her scary wolf dreams, will Aunt Tara know how to comfort her?

When dawn finally arrived, I treated myself to a morning of nothingness. Doing nothing is hard work! Today was my last day off before Salome comes home tomorrow. No more sleeping until the sun rises and no more quiet moments in the middle of the afternoon. Salome will latch onto me like a second skin. She'll probably bring home a whole new set of questions.

No sense sitting around killing time, I thought, *especially on a bright, clear morning like today.* I slipped over to Papa's workshop to let him know I would be taking a walk. It's a good thing I watched where I was going, or I'd have tripped over a pile of debris he'd left lying right in front of the entryway. My father is the most creative person I know, but he's blind to clutter. Mama used to help him organize his storage areas and was a pro at keeping his floor free of junk. "You can't sell beautiful pottery from a pigsty, Hiram," she'd remind him.

The steady hum of his potter's wheel was a familiar comfort. When I was little, Mama and I would sit quietly beside Papa, watching him turn balls of wet clay into works of art. Today I left him alone, though. A layer of curly scraps littered the floor under Papa's workbench, but I didn't dare poke around with a broom until he was finished for the day. I headed to a storage area instead—a little-used corner where dust-covered castoffs sat like weary soldiers atop a long, narrow table. I lifted each item carefully, dusting as I worked my way through the neglected wares.

There I found a vase—a remarkable creation with a delicate, curled lip and rounded sides. It was rough compared to Papa's other work, and it didn't have a pretty border. No flowers or vines. No delicate swirls. Nothing. Still, I liked it. It would make a perfect vase for our mystery bouquets—much nicer than the old stained container I'd borrowed from the shed. I coughed to get Papa's attention. "Papa, could I have this old vase?" I asked. "It looks like nobody ever came for it."

His shoulders slouched and the wheel came to an abrupt stop. "Put it back where you found it, Deborah."

"But it's perfect, Papa. I was thinking—"

"Please. Put it back." His jaw tightened while he waited for me to respond.

I placed the vase back on its shelf in the corner, but not before I noticed a marking across its bottom: an H and an E entwined like two strands of ivy. Hiram and Eritha—Papa and Mama? *If this vase could speak, what would it say?*

Papa wiped his gritty hands on his apron. "I think you've dusted enough for one day, honey. Thank you."

"I'm going for a walk," I said quietly. "I just thought you'd want to know."

My path led past Ori's house, down the road past a stately row of palm trees. Ziva's older brother says that if you stand still near the base of the trees at night, you'll hear mice scurrying up and down the trunks and playing tag on the fronds.

Two women waved to me. A goatskin bottle hung from a wooden frame between them. They rocked the bottle back and forth, checking every so often to see whether their cream had thickened into butter. Watching them was like stepping back a few years, to watch Mama and Grandmother working together in the courtyard.

I continued on, paying no attention to how far I'd walked. My toe kicked something round and hard. Funny, I'd never noticed a pomegranate tree on our street before. Whoever invented pockets deserves an award; I stuffed two pomegranates in each pocket and turned around for the walk home. From that moment on, everything changed.

An unfamiliar row of houses stretched down a hillside, connected by a worn wall. My house isn't fancy like the mansions on the west side, but I'd never seen anything quite like the sight before me.

"Hello!" called a girl about my age. I returned her greeting and almost hurried by, but she sailed into the street and met me head-on. "My name's Anna. What's yours?" Anna's eyes sparkled like someone who had discovered a hidden gift. "Where do you live?"

"Down there," I said. "At least I think it's down there. I think I might be lost."

Anna shoved her hands into a faded blue tunic that looked like it had been patched one time too many. "Want to stay awhile?" she asked. "You can meet my family."

"No ... I mean, not today. I need to get home. Tomorrow's my papa's birthday, and I have to bake him a cake."

Anna's face dropped. "My mama won't turn me loose in the kitchen yet," she laughed. "I caught the last cake on fire! Can you believe that?"

Anna was my kind of girl! I liked her spunk. "Well, at least come and meet my mama," she said. Without waiting for an answer, she turned and led the way up a sloping courtyard into a tiny house.

It was hard not to stare. Anna's house was made of mud brick like mine, except hers looked ancient. Splotches of patched areas were starting to peel and flake. *One good rain and this place will collapse,* I thought. Thankfully, we don't get much rain in Jericho.

A strong musty smell permeated every corner of the main room. The odor was so heavy, I coughed to relieve my itching throat. Empty except for a long mat—probably used in place of a table— the room held only a couple of dilapidated chairs. Five sleeping mats had been rolled and stacked off to one side. Anna's house was noticeably dark, in spite of sunshine leaking through holes here and there.

A cheery woman with dancing blue eyes motioned me into a cooking area, where a scrawny goat lay on a heap of straw in the corner. "He looks like my goat Mikko," I said, "except Mikko is fat and sassy and spoiled rotten. She's old and doesn't give milk anymore."

"Not this one," laughed Anna's mama. "She doesn't have the luxury of refusing. She's our only source of milk."

Two sweaty little boys roared into the house, brushing past me as if they didn't notice me there. "Boys, where are your manners!" scolded their mother.

"Sorry," they said in unison. Turning to Anna, they whispered loud enough for me to hear, "Who's *she?*"...

Who is the girl in the kitchen?
Will she become best friends with Anna?
And will the vase speak?

Find out what has happened when you read
Deborah's Secret Journal.

Releasing September 2004.

The Word at Work . . .

What would you do if you wanted to share God's love with children on the streets of your city? That's the dilemma David C. Cook faced in 1870s Chicago. His answer was to create literature that would capture children's hearts.

Out of those humble beginnings grew a worldwide ministry that has used literature to proclaim God's love and disciple generation after generation. Cook Communications Ministries is committed to personal discipleship—to helping people of all ages learn God's Word, embrace his salvation, walk in his ways, and minister in his name.

Opportunities—and Crisis

We live in a land of plenty—including plenty of Christian literature! But what about the rest of the world? Jesus commanded, "Go and make disciples of all nations" (Matt. 28:19) and we want to obey this commandment. But how does a publishing organization "go" into all the world?

There are five times as many Christians around the world as there are in North America. Christian workers in many of these countries have no more than a New Testament, or perhaps a single shared copy of the Bible, from which to learn and teach.

We are committed to sharing what God has given us with such Christians.

A vital part of Cook Communications Ministries is our international outreach, Cook Communications Ministries International (CCMI). Your purchase of this book, and of other books and Christian-growth products from Cook, enables CCMI to provide Bibles and Christian literature to people in more than 150 languages in 65 countries.

Cook Communications Ministries is a not-for-profit, self-supporting organization. Revenues from sales of our books, Bible curricula, and other church and home products not only fund our U.S. ministry, but also fund our CCMI ministry around the world. One hundred percent of donations to CCMI go to our international literature programs.

. . . **Around the World**

CCMI reaches out internationally in three ways:

· Our premier International Christian Publishing Institute (ICPI) trains leaders from nationally led publishing houses around the world to develop evangelism and discipleship materials to transform lives in their countries.

· We provide literature for pastors, evangelists, and Christian workers in their national language. We provide study helps for pastors and lay leaders in many parts of the world, such as China, India, Cuba, Iran, and Vietnam.

· We reach people at risk—refugees, AIDS victims, street children, and famine victims—with God's Word. CCMI puts literature that shares the Good News into the hands of people at spiritual risk—people who might die before they hear the name of Jesus and are transformed by his love.

Word Power, God's Power

Faith Kidz, RiverOak, Honor, Life Journey, Victor, NexGen — every time you purchase a book produced by Cook Communications Ministries, you not only meet a vital personal need in your life or in the life of someone you love, but you're also a part of ministering to José in Colombia, Humberto in Chile, Gousa in India, or Lidiane in Brazil. You help make it possible for a pastor in China, a child in Peru, or a mother in West Africa to enjoy a life-changing book. And because you helped, children and adults around the world are learning God's Word and walking in his ways.

Thank you for your partnership in helping to disciple the world. May God bless you with the power of his Word in your life.

For more information about our international ministries, visit www.ccmi.org.

*A*dditional copies of this book are available
from your local bookstore.

——➤◆◄——

If you have enjoyed this book, or if it has impacted
your life, we would like to hear from you.

——➤◆◄——

Please contact us at:

Cook Communications Ministries

4050 Lee Vance View

Colorado Springs, CO 80918

Or by e-mail at cookministries.com